Death Beneath the Sphinx

An Ancient Egyptian Mystery

William G. Collins

Death Beneath the Sphinx

ISBN 10: 1542764599

ISBN 13: 9781542764599

Cover design: Chris Holmes whiterabbitgraphix.com

Other Novels by the Author in the Cat Series

Murder in Pharaoh's Palace

Death Beneath the Sphinx

Murder at Abu Simbel

Other Novels by the Author about Egypt

Behind the Golden Mask

Prince of the Nile

In A Land of Dreams

To Catch the Wind

Murder by the Gods

ACKNOWLEDGEMENTS

Special appreciation to two writing groups:

The Florida Writers Association's

Daytona Area Fiction Writers and

The Port Orange Scribes Second Edition.

Especially Veronica H. Hart, leader, and

Dr. Robert Hart, Chris Holmes, Lois Gerber,

Amanda Alexander, Matthew Hudson, Joan

King, Marie Brack, Carolyn Wade, Joyce

Senatro, Diana Boilard.

And to my wife, Evangeline Rose, my

Muse and first editor.

PREFACE

People around the world call the enormous statue in front of the Great Pyramid, the Sphinx. However, to the Ancient Egyptians, it was the Great Lion, symbol of the Pharaohs, and Horus of the Horizon. The Greeks named it the Sphinx after they entered Egypt in 332 B.C.E., and it is the largest surviving sculpture from the ancient world. Therefore, in this work, the sacred river is just the "river," and not the Nile. The cataracts are simply "rapids" or "waterfalls."

The story takes place during the reign of Pharaoh Khafre, son of Khufu, builder of the Great Pyramid. It is the "golden age" of the Fourth Dynasty in approximately 2570 B.C.E. Khafre succeeded his brother Djedefre who died under questionable circumstances. His dismantled pyramid, begun eight kilometers distant from the Giza plateau has recently been re-discovered.

Egyptian cats, known as Mau, were perhaps earliest of all domestic cats. They were important to the Egyptians because they helped rid the land of rats, known by physicians of that day to carry disease and death. Worshipped by their masters, these feline pets were often mummified and interred with them in their tombs.

This is the story of one cat who became involved in the history of the Pharaohs.

"Dogs believe they are human.
Cats believe they are God."

CHAPTER ONE

The cat yawned and shifted her weight. She liked to sleep on the right paw of the Great Lion where the warmth of the sun lingered in the stones on that side of the great beast. Her dark stripes had just begun to show. Something moved below and caught her attention. She lifted her head and then sat up.

"Shh. Quiet."

"Where are we going, Nubuti?"

The giant statue guarding the pyramid towered over the two figures, stretching out its full length on the sand. In the moonlight, crickets chirped as if to answer the scrunching of the sand beneath the intruders' sandals. Bats, frightened from hidden recesses beneath the statue, flew up in a burst of flapping leathery wings. The shorter of the two men stopped and leaned against the lion, the stone surface radiating the warmth of the day's sunlight.

"Tell me where we're going, 'Buti, or I go no further."

"Listen, Hui, you agreed to come with me. Now be silent." Hui served as aide to the Lord Chamberlain, while Nubuti served the commanding officer of the Royal Guards and lived in the military barracks.

A night owl screeched as it swooped down toward them, hunting an easy meal. To escape it, a small creature leapt off the lion and landed on the shoulder of the taller of the two.

Nubuti yelled in fear and then in pain as small sharp claws dug into his shoulder. Scared out of his wits he tried to knock it off. "Eww, Hui! Gods, what is it?"

Hui laughed. "It's only a cat. Here, let me take it." He lifted the animal carefully off his friend and cradled it in his arms. "There, there, little one. What are you doing out here?"

"Miuuuu. . ."

"Get rid of it," Nubuti said. "I don't like cats."

"Too bad. I do. Don't anger the cat goddess."

Nubuti rubbed his sore shoulder, scowling. "Let's go. The Temple of the Horizon is up ahead."

"But no one will be there," Hui protested. "It's the middle of the night."

"Quiet. I know what I'm doing. Keep up."

Hui pet the cat on the head and it purred in response. Its distinctive stripes easily seen in the moon's light. "You know what will happen if the guards find us out here. They'll think we're grave robbers and will kill us without asking questions."

"The guards are probably asleep," Nubuti said. "We're almost there."

A creature slithered across their path, its scaly skin glittering with pale blue light. This time it was Hui's turn to jump. He shuddered and had difficulty speaking. "I…hate…snakes." They gave it a wide berth and resumed their quest.

Bright moonlight on the slender columns of the temple cast dense black shadows over the sand.

Hui whispered, "I can't see anyone." His voice still quivered from his snake encounter. He had been here once before when Pharaoh Khafre laid the corner stone of the temple to honor Khufu the Great, his father. Oil lamps flickered inside but the young men didn't see anyone.

Nubuti led his friend up the steps and into the large rectangular hall dominated by a life-like statue of Pharaoh.

Hui became even more anxious and a shudder ran down his spine. It was unnerving to stand in the presence of the image of Khafre, the living god.

"Nubuti," a man's voice growled out of the shadows. "Where have you been? It will be light soon."

Nubuti nodded to the priest as he emerged from the darkness. Dressed in the traditional white robe of his profession, he lit his way with an oil lamp carried at chest height. The old man's shaved head sparkled with reflected light from the flickering lamp. He walked to the back of the sanctuary, opened a wooden door and ushered his visitors inside. A simple table and a few chairs filled the center of the room which smelled of incense and lamp oil. He motioned for them to take a seat.

Hui sighed, putting his feet up on a spare chair.

"Where is it?" the priest asked.

"Only if you have the gold," Nubuti said.

The priest reached inside his robe and placed two gold coins on the table. "As agreed."

Nubuti took a gold dagger from his tunic and placed it next to the coins.

The priest picked it up and examined it closely. "Excellent. This will do nicely."

Nubuti said, "No one must ever know how you got it, Lord Roi."

The priest smiled and nodded.

The cat meowed and leapt out of Hui's arms. It landed on the table and startled the priest who pointed the dagger at the animal.

Hui jumped and scooped up the cat protectively. "Apologies, my Lord. We found her up by the Great Lion."

Nubuti said, "Have we finished here?"

The priest stood, his pleased expression evident in the dim light. "Take your gold and be gone."

Nubuti nodded, not quite a bow. "Come on, Hui." His friend followed him back out into the long dark hall. The moon helped them find their way through the forest of polished columns.

"Why did the priest need the dagger, 'Buti?"

His friend didn't respond but walked on in silence until they reached the river and the canoe borrowed earlier.

They climbed aboard and Nubuti said, "Don't worry about it. The priest told me he wanted to give it as a gift during the celebration of the princess's seventeenth summer feast."

"Oh, really? But why did we have to bring it in the middle of the night?"

Nubuti grabbed a paddle and frowned. "I don't know, but I got paid and need the money. Let's go."

Hui sat down in the back of the canoe and put the cat on his lap. Grasping his paddle, he used it to ease them out into the current. It would take half the time going back thanks to the strong current carrying them north. Ahead of them came the snorting of a hippo and Hui turned his paddle to steer the canoe around the danger. Usually, water-horses slept close to shore at night, but he knew how unpredictable they could be.

The cat mewled, and Hui stopped paddling a moment to pet it.

Nubuti grumbled. "Keep rowing."

Hui spoke to the cat. "Easy, baby. I don't need a little ball of teeth, claws and flying fur. We're almost there." He plunged his oar once again into the water.

At the eastern shore, they left the canoe where they'd found it.

"See you in two days," Nubuti said.

"If the gods allow," Hui replied. He put the cat on his shoulders and began the walk home. A mangy dog barked at him on the way and he winced as the cat's claws dug into him. At the palace gate, the guards looked for the chamberlain's small brand on Hui's bicep and let him pass. He usually covered it with a wide gold band to discourage people from learning where he worked. It was an honor to serve such an important official, but when people found out the identity of his master, they often tried to use him to influence the king's Right Hand.

In his room at the chamberlain's villa, Hui undressed and washed his hands and face in the ceramic basin of water. He toweled off and stretched his arms as if to touch the ceiling. He kept himself fit, and women said his face and deep voice pleased them. Hui had experienced twenty summers and was thin and of medium height. Well-developed muscles gave him the appearance of a warrior. He kept his hair cropped, and his greenish eyes captured people's attention—more blue than green, they hinted at an ancestor from a country far to the north.

He bunched up his blanket to make a bed for his new furry friend. "What were you doing out on the Great Lion, little lady? There's no way you could swim across the river. You'd have been some crocodile's treat."

"Meowrrr..."The cat sniffed around the blanket, yawned, arched her back and dug her claws into it. Her purring grew louder.

Hui blew out the oil lamp and lay on his bed. "Good night, little one."

The cat responded by snuggling up to him and putting her paw on his cheek. Her soft purring lulled them both to sleep.

A loud and insistent knock on his door awakened him. Sunlight beamed through the window. Yawning, he leapt out of bed, opened the door and admitted his master. Lord Phanes' hair was pure white and his Adam's apple wobbled when he talked.

"Long night?"The Lord Chamberlain asked.

"Yes, my Lord. My friend, Nubuti, took me on a wild journey. We didn't return until early in the morning."

His master grinned, and crossed his arms. "Oh? Wine and women, then?"

Hui shook his head with embarrassment. “No, my Lord, nothing as good as that. Nubuti wanted to do a favor for someone. All I came back with is this cat.”

“Ah, and such a beauty. What a splendid color.”

The cat jumped off the bed and rubbed against Lord Phanes shins. “Meow,” she sang, and then began purring.

“She certainly has good taste,” the older man said. “Come, Hui. Pharaoh needs us. We will have a busy day.”

In the royal palace, the sun-god Ra sent his golden fingers to awaken Princess Rekhetre. When they caressed her face, she opened her eyes, stretched her arms and sat up. A slight breeze carried the sweet fragrance of lotus flowers blooming in the pool outside her window.

“Ah, you’re awake, Highness,” her lady-in-waiting said. “Your bath is ready. Did you sleep well?”

The princess smiled. “Oh yes, Benemba. I dreamed about someone special.”

“Oh? I hope the prince is someone your father approves.”

The princess laughed. “Oh, rubbish, Benemba, you old frog! I’m going to choose him myself.”

The older woman shook her head. “Come, your bath awaits. His Majesty is expecting you this morning.”

The daughter of Pharaoh left her bed and walked to the tiled bathing room. As she stepped down into the large copper tub, two servants knelt beside it and bathed her with warm scented water. She leaned back and thought of her love. Captain Paru came from a noble family in the former capital of Avaris. Tall and muscular, he had experienced twenty-three summers. She loved to run her fingers through his short bronze hair and had fallen in love with him from the moment they first met. She knew it was wrong. Her whole life had prepared her for the day she would marry the man her father chose for her, but one could not predict or control the heart.

Later, dressed in one of her finest pleated gowns, she walked to the family dining room and found her younger brother, Dua, finishing his morning meal.

"It is about time, Great Swan," he said, speaking formally, with the royal's distinctive rhythm to his words. He only called her that when he wanted to annoy her. He stood a head taller than his sister, and wore his princely braid to the right of his otherwise shaved head.

Hettie smiled at him, raising her eyebrows. "I am not fighting with you, Dua. It is too nice a day."

Prince Dua laughed. "Aha. You have received another letter?"

"Be quiet, little monkey," she hissed. "Do you want father to hear?"

"Hear what?" Pharaoh Khafre said entering the dining room.

His son and daughter stood and bowed their heads. He motioned for them to resume their places.

Prince Duaenre spoke first. "It is nothing, Father. I like to tease her."

Pharaoh said, "Not when I am present." He walked over to the wall panels and opened them to let in the morning light. He turned to admire his daughter. "You appear in a pleasant mood, Hettie."

"Yes, Father. Who would not be pleasant today? It is a beautiful morning."

"True. Your mother pointed that out to me a few moments ago."

The princess loved her father, king of the world. The sun glistened off his head indicating his barbers had already been at work. She thought of him as old since he had lived to see forty summers, but knew of his strength and fitness when sparring with his guards. He wore the necklace of his ancestors on his bare chest, as well as the short white pleated kilt of a warrior. A servant stood against the wall holding the king's menes headdress. He would put it on his majesty when he left the royal apartment.

Once seated, Pharaoh said, "Hettie, you will come to the Hall of Audiences today when the sun is at its zenith. Your mother will join us."

Hettie swallowed hard and cleared her throat. "Yes, Father." She felt fear. If he was calling her to the council chambers, did it mean he might have already chosen someone for her to marry? Could it be Paru? She had spoken to him enough about the handsome officer. But what if it's not? Surely her father loved her enough to make a good match with someone important—a handsome man, a good man. She shivered inside as she thought of what it would be like to be married to Paru. Would he carry her in his arms on their first night and kiss her firmly? What if it wasn't him? Her hands became sweaty and she picked up one of the small linen cloths and dried them.

Dua left the table first, and the princess followed after, bowing her head to her father.

Back in her room, she called for Sinhue, the only scribe she trusted. "I will write a letter to the Captain of the Guard. Deliver it to him personally." She dictated the letter and admired Sinhue's script, much more beautiful than her own. Educated in the palace, the princess could read and write as well as he, but it made her feel important to be able to speak the words and watch them appear on the papyrus at someone else's hand.

Sinhue read the letter back to her. She nodded in approval and he said, "The gods will bless me for being the go-between for such great lovers."

She giggled. "Leave us, you mischievous ruffian. Make sure you are not followed."

The scribe grinned, bowed his head politely, and left.

Hui followed his master, the Lord Chamberlain into the study next to the Hall of Audiences. With the elderly man's permission, he carried the cat with him and put her down on the desk. She sat staring at the two men with her penetrating chartreuse eyes.

The room smelled of dust, ink and ancient paper. Rolled papyrus scrolls filled large square niches built into the walls on each side of the office. Hui helped the Chamberlain put on his ornate collar of office which they stored in a small cupboard.

"This morning, his majesty is going to handle a delicate matter," Phanes said.

Hui liked the fact that his mentor shared the cases Pharaoh would handle in the day. "A delicate matter, my Lord?"

Phanes rubbed his hand over his head. "Yes, Hui. Have you met Prince Kasmut?"

"No, Master."

"Pharaoh must make his decision about his daughter this morning."

Hui scowled. "You don't mean he's chosen this prince for Hettie?"

"I'm afraid so. He hasn't told me officially, but I know the king wants her to marry someone from his side of the family."

"But, we both know the princess has already chosen someone."

Phanes frowned. "Go on."

"I only ask if the princess must marry someone she doesn't know or love?"

Phanes seated himself, and the cat moved to him. He scratched along her back, making her purr. "Pharaoh's word is law, especially when it concerns family."

A knock on the door called Hui to answer. He opened it and Lord Phanes recognized the caller. He stood and walked to the door. Bowing his head he said, "Prince Kasmut. Welcome, Highness."

Hui bowed too and studied the man entering the small room. He was an older man, probably having seen forty summers, with considerable gray hair and a protruding stomach.

"May we speak privately, Lord Chamberlain?"

"Of course, Highness." Phanes made a small wave of his hand, and Hui picked up his cat and left.

Hui hurried down the hall to the room next door. Finding it empty, he closed the door and put the cat down. He stood beside the stone wall and put his head near one of the joints where the mortar had loosened. He removed a chip enabling him to hear every word in the chamberlain's office.

"How may I help you, Highness?" Phanes asked.

"You may not know, my Lord, but I've come to take the princess in marriage."

"Pharaoh has agreed?"

"Yes, my Lord. I count on you to prepare all the necessary legal documents."

Hui moved from the wall and sat on the only chair in the room. "Well, little lady," he said to the cat. "I have a good friend who's going to be upset."

CHAPTER TWO

Captain Paru opened the letter from the palace, and instructed the scribe to wait. When he finished reading it, he laughed and folded it. "That will be all, Sinhue."

The scribe nodded, and left.

Paru smiled. His love wanted to see him today after her audience with the king. She would be going to the Great Temple of Horus in the center of Memphis and he would be in charge of her escort. At the end of the religious service, the high priest would lead her to the garden in the temple enclosure where he could join her. They would be alone at last. The priest had kept their secret for several months and Paru knew the holiest man in the kingdom could be trusted.

"Nubuti," Paru called to his household servant, "I'm needed at the palace for a special audience. Lay out my clean kilt."

"Yes, Captain."

Paru entered his bedchamber and removed his clothes. Nubiti brought him a large basin of water and towels so the officer could wash before dressing. As the son of the governor of the northern Nome of Awen, Paru had ambitions for a higher position in Pharaoh's army.

Putting on his loincloth and finely woven, thigh-length white kilt, he added a wide leather belt to hold his short sword. He kept a small marble bust Hettie gave him on his bedside table. It had been love from the first moment they met. Her horse had bolted during a routine ride with her father, and Paru had raced after her and managed to rein in the mare. When he helped her dismount, a thrill coursed through his body from being near her. She told him later she had experienced it too. He kissed the carved image and put it back.

Placing the warrior's cloth nemes on his head, he left the bedchamber and headed for the door. "I don't know what my plans are for this evening," he told Nubuti.

"Very well, sir. There'll be beer and bread in the cupboard in case you come in late."

"Good." Paru turned and left.

Lord Phanes was anxious about the Princess's audience with Pharaoh. It was almost midday and he had difficulty motivating the ambassadors to be brief. He waved his hand, calling for his aide.

Hui approached. "Tell the ambassador from Cyprus to come back tomorrow. His majesty will receive no one else."

"Yes, my Lord." Hui bowed and returned to the large waiting room adjacent to the Hall of Audiences. Hui knew that Lord Phanes hoped he would take his place one day. With no children of his own, he considered Hui as a son. But the king could choose anyone to be chamberlain, and life at court was never certain.

Pharaoh raised his hand and Lord Phanes struck the polished limestone floor with his staff three times, one for each of the three principal gods of Egypt. He raised his voice and announced, "Pharaoh Khafre, Son of the Great Khufu and the god Horus has finished dispensing his wisdom. Bow before him."

The ambassador from Byblos bowed low before the ruler of the world and the chamberlain then led him out of the hall. Upon his return, Pharaoh stepped down from the throne and stretched his arms and legs. He shook his head from side to side to loosen his neck muscles and smiled at his friend.

"Is it time for the Princess?"

"Yes, Majesty, but you have a moment for a little wine and a piece of honey cake. I've placed them in your antechamber. Semi, the cupbearer, is there to taste the wine."

"Excellent. I grow weary of ambassadors. They talk too much, and that one from Byblos is as mad as a bag of frogs!"

The chamberlain burst out laughing, and the king joined in. They had known each other since they were boys when Phanes' father was Pharaoh Khufu's chamberlain. They grew up in and around the palace. In the privacy of the anteroom, Pharaoh allowed Phanes to sit with him and share the refreshment. It was an honor few could enjoy, usually only family members could sit in the royal presence.

"Will my son be joining us?" Pharaoh asked.

"No, Majesty. Prince Duaenre is with his regiment on an exercise in the desert. He won't be back for two days."

Pharaoh nodded. "It is just as well. He may not be pleased with what is about to happen."

Queen Persenet smiled as her daughter entered the family's private apartment. Hettie's mother had seen thirty-five summers and her beauty still enchanted her subjects. She refused to put on one of the wigs preferred by the court, and chose instead to wear her hair cut short with bangs. No wrinkles marred her face and the heritage of her Thinis ancestors was evident in her smooth alabaster skin which was the envy of her young ladies-in-waiting.

"Ah, you have chosen the turquoise gown," the queen said. "Your father will be pleased."

Hettie smiled and bowed her head respectfully. "I am happy you like it, Mother. What is this all about?"

"In good time, Hettie. Your father will explain."

"But Mother. . ."

Her mother waved her hand. "We must go. He's waiting for us."

The princess clenched her teeth making her jaw stick out a little. She had always done it as a child when she didn't get her way and it made her mother laugh. Hettie couldn't help smiling. "Very well, Majesty. I can never stay angry with you."

Her mother took her by the arm and they walked out of the royal apartment and down the long polished corridor of the palace. Captain Paru waited outside the apartment to escort them. Hettie kept her eyes straight ahead.

The chamberlain stood at the large golden doors leading into the Audience Hall. "Your Majesty," Phanes said, bowing to the queen and princess. "Welcome, Highness, his Majesty awaits." He motioned for the guards to open the doors and they walked through together. Phanes struck the polished granite floor again with his staff of office and spoke in a clear, loud voice. "Behold Queen Persenet, Principal Wife of Pharaoh Khafre, and Daughter of Iset—Mother of Egypt. Fall down before her."

Those in the hall prostrated themselves on the floor before the queen.

Fragrant cedar wood covered the walls of the enormous room. Colorful representations of Pharaoh and his ancestors painted on the white ceiling brought the room to life. Nearly transparent linen draperies embroidered with gold thread bearing the names of Pharaoh and his queen, hung behind the thrones.

Phanes struck the floor with his staff again. "Behold Princess Rekhetre, Daughter of their Majesties and Priestess of Iset our holy Mother of Egypt."

The queen and her daughter walked forward. Pharaoh stepped down and welcomed his queen at the bottom of the steps. He extended his arm and led her up to her throne.

The chamberlain gestured for the princess to remain in front of the steps. Pharaoh Khafre and the queen seated themselves and the king raised his hand giving permission for those present to stand.

A small group of noblemen stood to the left of their majesties. Hettie didn't recognize any of them. The muscles of her stomach drew tighter and she bit down on her lower lip to steel herself for what was to come.

Pharaoh said, "Daughter, it is with great pleasure that we welcome you today. You make us proud by the way you have grown and served our kingdom. What we are about to do will secure peace in our Kingdom, and you will serve us well."

Hettie glanced at her mother whose stoic expression warned her not to react.

"Prince Kasmut," Pharaoh called. "You have our permission to approach."

The rotund man, wearing a crown of gray hairs on his balding head, walked toward the throne and bowed before their majesties.

"Daughter, this is our cousin, Prince Kasmut. His father and mine were born in the same year."

"Prince," she said bowing.

He, however, didn't return the courtesy, but said simply, "Your Highness."

Pharaoh turned to her. "Dearest Princess, it is our decision that you marry Kasmut in a month's time at the Feast of the Full Moon. Your mother is also pleased with our decision."

Hettie's blood ran cold. She turned to her mother whose eyes stared straight ahead—her face as rigid as granite. Hettie struggled to keep the tears from coming, and bit down on her tongue. She bowed to her father, but found it difficult to find the words to respond. Finally, she replied just above a whisper, "Majesty, I am always pleased to do your will. I pray the gods will approve this union."

"Excellent," Pharaoh stood and walked down the steps and took his daughter's hand. He placed it in Prince Kasmut's. "With our blessing, our two families will grow close again."

"I pray it will be so, Majesty," the prince replied.

The queen stood, walked down the steps, took her daughter by the arm and wordlessly led her out of the hall.

After mother and daughter returned to the family apartment, Captain Paru and his guards took their positions outside the doors. He walked some distance away down the hall to an open area providing access to the garden. He slammed his fist against the wall and exclaimed, "By the gods! I've lost her."

Hui overheard him and approached. "What did Pharaoh say?"

Paru knew Hui could be trusted. Many of his men told him so. The captain was so frustrated he needed to speak to someone. Moving to an alcove where they wouldn't be overheard, he told Hui everything.

When he finished, Hui frowned. "Who is this prince, anyway?"

"No one knows him. And look at him! He's as old as my father."

Hui nodded. "I must admit, he would not be my choice for the princess. I've known her all my life and this will break her heart."

"We'll have to run away, Hui. There's no other way." Paru stood, his face flushed, the muscles of his jaw pulsing in anger. He turned and slammed his fist into the wooden lattice, breaking it into small pieces.

Hui shook his head. "Calm down, my friend. Didn't you tell me you are meeting her at the temple in a little while? Talk to her, reassure her of your love."

Paru moaned. "It's going to be hard to hide our feelings for each other. We only have a month to find a solution, Hui. Can we trust you with our secret and will you help us?"

"Of course, Captain. May I speak to Lord Phanes about this? I won't mention your name, only that the princess loves someone else. He has a good mind and may be able to find a solution."

"Very well, but Pharaoh will kill us if he finds out. Please, Hui, no one can know."

"I understand. I'll also try to find out the reasons behind Pharaoh's decision."

The two men nodded to each other and parted ways.

Later, at home, Hui finally got the courage to speak to his mentor about Paru's plight. When he finished, he saw the look of horror and disbelief on the chamberlain's face.

"I can't betray his majesty, Hui. He trusts me as a friend. If I were to help Paru, he would have to execute me and you as well."

Hui shook his head and got up from the table where they had been sitting. "I am sorry, my Lord. You are my father, and I owe you my greatest respect. However, I plan to involve myself in helping Paru and the princess, with or without your approval. Forgive me, my Lord."

The old man's face darkened as he considered Hui's words. Clearing his throat, he spoke just above a whisper. "My boy, if you had one great weakness, it would be this. You've always been too kind, willing to help anyone who came to you."

Hui nodded, too moved to speak.

"Let me sleep on this, my son."

Lord Ameni, the High Priest of the god Horus—protector of the royal family, led the princess into the temple garden. Captain Paru stood at attention by the fountain. The couple waited for the priest to leave before embracing and Hettie began to sob uncontrollably. Paru held her. Neither of them could speak. They moved to a granite bench near the pool and held hands.

Paru couldn't sit, and stood facing her. "I'm not going to let him have you, Hettie. I'll break you out of this palace and set you free. I'm so angry I could kill anyone who comes between us."

Hettie let him vent his frustration and squeezed his hand until he finally sat down.

Paru continued. "I've made the acquaintance of someone who might help us. I'm sure you know him. It's Hui, the Lord Chamberlain's aide. He knows about us."

"Oh, Hui, of course. I trust him too. He is like another brother. We grew up in the palace. But I fear for his life too, if father finds out."

"I'm desperate, my love. We must leave Egypt. We'll go north and find a safe place on the coast. That old man cannot have you!"

She frowned, and stood beside him. Turning away for a moment, she ran her hand over some jasmine blossoms. "He *is* old, isn't he, and fat! What is father thinking? I had been taught that Egyptian princesses married other kings to make peace treaties. But to marry an old cousin for no other reason than to bring our families together is not what I deserve."

"Listen, beloved. We can meet at Hui's place. He lives with the chamberlain and it would mean Lord Phanes would know. Hui says he is like a father to him and wouldn't tell the secret to anyone—especially the king."

Hettie's voice began to tremble. "It's all so sudden. In one day, my life has changed. If I defy my family, I will die, and you with me, Paru, and to involve Hui and Phanes, it's all frightening."

He embraced her and they sat on the bench and were silent for a time. She wiped away a stray tear. "Very well. I'll come tonight dressed in my servant's clothes, but no palace guards can know about it. I'll take old Geta, the chief cook with me. He is big and strong. He'll only know that I'm visiting Phanes on an important matter. He'll protect me."

"Horus protect you," Paru scanned around the garden for prying eyes again before embracing her. They kissed passionately and then took leave of each other.

Outside, on the veranda, Lord Phanes sat in his favorite chair enjoying the evening breeze.

The cat meandered out and rubbed against his legs before jumping up and settling on his lap.

"Hui, this cat has taken over the house," the elderly man said.

"I know, my Lord. I'm afraid she's adopted us, and there is nothing we can do." He grinned at the chamberlain and shrugged. "It is the will of the goddess." Pausing a moment, he added, "We'll have to call her something."

Another moment of silence passed between them as Lord Phanes continued to pet the cat.

Hui said, "She's domineering and yet affectionate—curious and then content to lie there for a long time. She thinks she's in charge of everything."

Phanes laughed. "Sounds like a goddess to me."

Hui scratched his head. "Hmm. . .a goddess? Let's name her for our mother goddess—Iset."

"Iset," Phanes repeated." It's the more ancient name for the goddess."

The cat's ears perked up and she sat on the chamberlain's lap. She cocked her head when he said her name. "Iset, is that you?"

"Meowrrr..." The cat reached out with her soft paw and touched the man's chin.

"Come, Iset, would you like some food?"

The cat jumped down and followed him to the kitchen. He gathered up some small river perch he brought home from the palace kitchen and placed them on a tin plate on the floor.

She sniffed them and looked up at him. "Meowll..."Then, she began to purr as loudly as a boy drumming his fingers on the table. She moved her head from side to side as she chewed.

The brass door knocker abruptly sounded—demanding their attention. Hui walked to the front door and opened it. "Ah, Captain, come in."

Wearing a simple tunic, the officer followed Hui out onto the veranda where the chamberlain stood and welcomed him.

"I'm sorry, my Lord," Paru said. "You are our only hope. I didn't intend to upset your life with my problems, but I don't know who else to confide in."

"You are Hui's friend, Captain. That is enough."

"Thank you, my Lord. I only pray the princess will come," Paru said.

"She'll be here," Hui said. "You don't know her as well as I do. We used to help her sneak out all the time. She loved to sail one of the small feluccas up and down the river. Her father would have died if he'd seen the risks Hettie took."

Paru's eyebrows bent low over his eyes. "Hettie? *You* call her Hettie?"

"Yes, her family and friends do. She's always been called that."

"Of course, I understand."

Iset chose that moment to introduce herself to the captain. "Meowrrllll?"

"This is Iset," Hui said. "She's taken up residence here."

"If only she were the true spirit of the goddess. Our mother god could help us," Paru said.

An urgent knock on the door signaled another visitor. Hui rushed out and opened it. The princess stood there alone.

"Come in, friend," Hui said.

"Thank you." She entered the room and pulled back the hood of her cloak.

Paru rushed over and embraced her. Hui and the chamberlain walked back onto the veranda. Hui smiled at his mentor and Phanes nodded to him.

"Oh, to be young again, my boy," the old man said.

The princess walked outside and joined them. "To be young can also be painful, old friend."

"Of course, Highness. Forgive me. I didn't mean to make light of your situation."

"Thank you for letting us be in your home, my Lord. Is it possible you can help us?"

"Let me begin by saying, my Lady, that to marry for love is not always possible for the children of the gods. When your father married your mother, he hardly knew her—but look how their love has grown over the years."

The princess shook her head. "You don't understand, my Lord. Prince Kasmut has been married four times and his wives are all dead. His breath is foul, and he smells like a pig. I know too that there is insanity on that side of my father's family. I would rather die than marry him."

"Gods," Paru exclaimed. "I will not allow it."

"Indeed," Phanes said. He paused a moment. "If I am to put my life in danger and agree to help, you then must decide to leave Egypt, children. Cut all ties with everyone you hold dear. I have merchant friends who will take you to Tyre where there is a large colony of Egyptians. It's where Pharaoh's ships are built." He paused, and looked toward Hui. "Hui and I will have to follow at the same time. Your father will know we helped you and must put a price on our heads."

Paru paced the room. "But how will we live, my Lord? I can always find a position in the military, but it will be difficult for Hettie to live a commoner's life. It will not be a life fit for a princess."

"Ah," Phanes sighed. "But you will be with her, and she will feel like a princess. I know you will survive. Now you must take gold with you of course. Your friends can send more once you are safe and settled. Trust no one. There is a ship leaving in two days and I will book passage if that is your desire."

"Do so, my Lord," Hettie said. "We are grateful. Now I must go back. They'll be missing me."

Paru asked, "Can you let us have a few moments in private, my friends?"

"Of course," Phanes said. "It is time I retired."

The princess suddenly bent down. "Oh, who is this tapping on my toes?"

"Meowwwwl. . . ." Iset mewled, making the princess laugh.

"This is Iset, my Lady. A new member of our household," Hui said.

Hettie ran her hand along the cat's spine making her purr. "Well, Iset. I am one of her priestesses. You must pray to the goddess for us."

The door knocker struck again and made them all jump.

The princess whispered. "We mustn't be seen."

Hui looked around, his eyebrows raised. He set his mouth and said, "In here, you two," He led them into the chamberlain's study.

"Go to the door," Lord Phanes said.

Hui hurried to the front and when he opened the door, found a soldier standing there.

"I'm sorry, sir. I'm looking for Captain Paru. His servant, Nubuti thought he'd be here."

"Yes, wait there," Hui said, as he shut the door.

Paru opened the study door. "Who is it?"

"One of your men. Nubuti sent him."

"Very well, that means something's wrong." He left the door to the study ajar and walked to the front door and opened it. "What is it, Maku?"

"You must come, Captain. Prince Kasmut's been murdered!"

"What?"

"The royal party were on a visit to the newly finished temple of the Pyramid and a guard found the body beneath the Great Lion. He had been stabbed several times."

"Gods," Paru exclaimed. "Did they find who did it?"

"Well…" the soldier mumbled.

"Out with it Maku! Who killed him?"

"They found the dagger used to kill him."

Captain Paru's eyes widened in disbelief. "It's her cartouche! By the gods!"

The princess, hearing the mention of Prince Kasmut's name, moved to the front door. "What is it?" Her eyes stared in disbelief and then she appeared on the edge of hysteria. "That's my dagger."

CHAPTER THREE

Paru swore. "By Seth's foul breath! I must go with the sergeant. Hui, tell the Chamberlain."

"Of course," Hui said, his voice shaken as he closed the door. He and the princess went into the front room and told Lord Phanes what had happened.

Phanes put his hand across his chest as if in pain. "The gods are displeased. Who could have done this thing?"

Hettie's face had turned pale. She grasped the arms of the nearest chair and sank into it. "But how could it be *my* dagger?" Then, she groaned putting her hand on her forehead. "Oh, no."

“What is it, Highness?” Hui asked.

“For two days I have missed the dagger my father gave me. Someone took it from my room.” She wrung her hands “Who would do such a thing?”

Lord Phanes sat on a chair near her. “Someone who wants to implicate you in the murder, Highness.”

“But why? I did not know the prince. No one did.”

Hui interrupted. “You must return to the palace, Princess. They’ll be looking for you. I’ll accompany you.”

“Meowrr.” Iset jumped onto the princess’s lap and nudged her cheek into the young woman’s chest.

Hui couldn’t help smiling. “Look, Highness. She’s trying to comfort you.”

“We will bring her with us, Hui. Maybe the goddess will hear *her* prayers and help us.” She picked up Iset and carried the cat with her. Saying farewell to the chamberlain, she pulled up the hood of her cloak and walked to the door.

Before Hui shut it behind them, he said, “I’ll be back, Master.”

Phanes nodded and headed toward his bedchamber.

Hui escorted the princess back to the palace and helped her enter through a little known hidden passage in the garden behind the royal apartments.

Unable to stand still, Pharaoh paced back and forth in the reception room of his private apartment. His face was drawn and he raised one eyebrow higher than the other. He mumbled under his breath, "Where *is* she?" The large gold necklace of his late father swung back and forth on his bare chest. Without sandals, his heels thudded on the tile floor as he moved about.

"She must be in the palace, Majesty," Captain Paru said. "No one saw her leave. My men would not have allowed it."

"Agreed. Then find her. She must answer for what's happened."

"My men brought Prince Kasmut's body here, Majesty. I have the dagger to show you. It's been washed clean so you need not fear any curse of the gods upon it."

"Bring it."

Paru walked to his sergeant who held the murder weapon in a linen cloth. He handed it to the officer who approached the king. "Is this her Highness's, Great Pharaoh?"

Khafre lifted the cloth and picked up the dagger. "That is her cartouche. I gave this to her last year at her naming day celebration. It was her sixteenth summer. How did it get to Giza and the Great Lion?"

"Will you permit a question, Majesty?"

Pharaoh nodded, stopped pacing and folded his arms across his chest. "Go on."

"Why did Prince Kasmut go to the Great Pyramid? Wasn't it unusual for him to be there the day you announced his engagement to the princess?"

Pharaoh Khafre frowned. "I had not thought of it that way, Captain. The queen suggested the prince visit the new paintings in the memorial temple. We are about to dedicate it to my father's memory and Prince Kasmut readily agreed."

"I understand, Majesty," Paru said.

"We can talk about this later. Find my daughter."

Paru saluted, struck his chest with his fist, made an about face, and left the apartment.

As he and his aide walked down the polished corridor, Paru asked a question for which he already knew the answer. "Where can she have gone? She must be back in the palace by now."

Sergeant Nafi nodded, and Paru was pleased he did not in any way show by his expression that he had discovered the princess in the chamberlain's house. "Perhaps her attendants know, Captain."

"No, no. I've spoken to all of them. No one has seen her."

"Has seen whom?" a familiar voice said behind them.

"Highness," Paru exclaimed, his face brightening. "Thank the gods you're all right."

"What is wrong with you, Captain? Why would I *not* be all right?" She nodded ever so slightly to Nafi.

"Your father sent me to find you and he'll have my head if I don't bring you to him this instant."

"Oh, very well. But why do the palace staff seem so surprised to see me?"

"Everyone thought you were missing, Princess."

When they reached the king's apartment, Paru ordered the steward to let them in. "Tell his Majesty the princess is here." His sergeant remained in the hall.

Pharaoh walked toward them, his face the color of pomegranate. "Hettie! Where have you been?"

The princess didn't speak, but walked nonchalantly over to one of the divans and sat down. "In the stables Father, brushing Shu. I guess I was not paying attention to how long I stayed."

"The stables? By Seth's entrails," the king swore and then fell onto the closest divan exasperated.

Paru went down on one knee and bowed his head. "I've failed you, Great Pharaoh. I never thought to look in the stables."

"It is not his fault, Father," Hettie quickly insisted. "I did not tell anyone where I went. Now will you tell me what is wrong?"

Pharaoh shook his head and stared at the officer. "Return to your post, Captain. That is all."

Concerned about what Pharaoh might do, he glanced briefly at Hettie without acknowledgement, and left.

When Pharaoh finally calmed down, he instructed his daughter to sit on the divan opposite him. He ran his hand over his head as the color of his face finally returned to normal.

"Please tell me, Father."

Pharaoh pulled on his goatee. "While you were giving your attention to your horse, someone murdered your future husband."

The princess stood and feigned surprise. "What? That is horrible. How?"

"I am sorry, Hettie, but the 'how' is easy." He stood and walked into his bedchamber, returning with the gold dagger. "The killer pushed this into Kasmut's heart."

"But, it cannot be." She took the dagger and examined it carefully, but put it down when it dawned on her that it had just killed someone. "It disappeared two days ago, Father. My attendants searched everywhere for it."

"What?"

"Yes. Someone must have stolen it from my room. I love this dagger because you gave it to me. I sleep with it next to my bed. I felt lost when it went missing."

Pharaoh scowled. "Rekhetre, why is it that you are more disturbed over this dagger than to learn Kasmut is dead? Why did you not tell me days ago it was stolen?"

Hettie bit her lower lip, trying to hold back tears. "I loved the dagger, Father, because I love the one who gave it to me.

I did not love a man I did not know. How can I regret what I never lost? He was a horrible man, Majesty."

"That is enough, Hettie. I decide who you marry."

At that moment, Hettie's mother entered the front room. "I do not want to risk your anger, Husband, but give her some peace, Khafre. She has suffered a shock."

The look of displeasure on his wife's face ended his remarks. "Go with your mother. We will talk later."

The princess walked over and bowed her head to him before kissing him on the cheek. The gesture so unnerved him, he turned and walked out onto the veranda.

Hui let Iset ride on his shoulder as he walked home from the palace. Instead of going directly to his adopted father's house, he walked to Captain Paru's quarters in the military barracks. When he knocked, Nubuti came to the door. His eyes widened when he found Hui standing there.

"What do you want?" he grumbled.

"Why'd you do it?"

"Do what?"

"Kill the prince! Don't tell me you didn't, 'Buti. Paru showed the dagger to Pharaoh and the princess is suspect and could die."

"Go away." Nubuti tried to shut the door, but Hui pushed it open. Iset jumped down and ran inside.

"Tell me now. You know I have to report it to the captain."

"Don't be foolish, Hui. We didn't kill the prince. You and I provided the dagger. That's all."

"What do you mean 'you and I'? You told me it was an urgent matter and wanted me to come with you. You carried the dagger, remember, not me. I knew nothing about it. When the captain finds out, he'll arrest you."

"But you came with me, Hui. You're just as guilty."

"It will be your word against mine. Who will Pharaoh believe? He knows and trusts me. Why would he listen to you?"

Nubuti ignored him and sat down at the kitchen table. "I was forced to do it. I took you along as a witness. In case something happened to me, you would know I only carried the dagger, but did not kill anyone."

"What? Then who ordered the dagger?"

"I don't know. I received instructions by letter. They threatened my family in my village if I didn't do what they said."

Hui took the only other chair. "Why didn't you tell me?"

"I couldn't. Isn't it obvious?"

"Why did they choose such an insignificant prince to kill?"

"I don't know." Nubuti ran the point of the blade of a small knife under his fingernails.

Hui eyed the knife and his muscles tensed in case his friend lunged at him.

Nubuti's eyes were red, a sure sign he wasn't sleeping. Hui's presence obviously made Nubuti nervous. "Go, and leave me alone," Nubuti grumbled. "Tell no one."

Hui said, "I must tell Lord Phanes first thing in the morning." He looked around and called his cat. "Iset? Come, lady." He made a high-pitched squeak with his lips, and she came running. He picked her up and placed her on his shoulder. Without another word, he left Paru's house and headed home.

Hui shared with the chamberlain how he was able to get Hettie back into the palace, but chose to leave out the part about his visit with Nubuti.

"Paru will get to the bottom of it," the old man said.

As Hui got in bed, Iset jumped up and waited for him to settle down. She tiptoed onto his stomach and then his chest. She purred loudly and bent her head down and let something fall from her mouth.

"What is it?" He reached for the object and held it in his hand. Wiping her saliva off with the sheet, he held it closer to the light of the oil lamp.

"Sobek's scaly skin. It's a ruby. You've stolen a ruby." He lay back down and examined the gem more closely. Suddenly it dawned on him. "This was in Nubuti's room, wasn't it? What does it mean? If only you could talk." He scratched behind her ear, "Thank you, Iset. Good cat."

"Meowwww..."Then, lying down against his shoulder, she nudged him with her cheek.

The next morning, Pharaoh ordered Paru to take a brigade of guards to Giza. "I want answers, Captain."

"Yes, Majesty." Slapping his fist to his chest, he hurried out.

He and Sergeant Nafi sailed from Memphis in a felucca with eight royal guards. The boat with its triangular sail fought the current and Paru enjoyed breathing in the fresh air. His hand trailed along in the water as a small family of brown ducks swam past. His men talked animatedly among themselves about the murder and he looked away. A mile south of the Giza Plateau, touching the sky at the highest elevation, Pharaoh Djedefre's pyramid reminded Paru of another royal tragedy. Djedefre died mysteriously in a hunting accident and the family chose not to finish his pyramid, burying him in a tomb deep below the foundation instead.

His sergeant's voice called him back to the present. "Once we're in Giza, where do we start, Captain?"

"We begin with Lord Roi, senior priest of the temple. My friend Hui tells me he is in charge of the shrine Pharaoh built to honor his father."

"Why do *you* think she killed the prince?"

"*She* didn't kill him," Paru said. "I'll never believe that. From what I hear, no one liked him, except Pharaoh." He paused and spoke so only Nafi could hear. "You will do well to forget what you saw at the chamberlain's house."

Nafi nodded. "Understood."

"Watch out," one of the guards shouted. "Croc on your side, Sir."

Paru yanked his hand out of the water. The boat rocked a little as they felt the long reptile bump the side of the boat as it swam past. Paru made a face as the smell of death and rotting flesh on the beast reached them.

Nafi yelled, "Hold on tight, men. He's hoping for a quick meal."

The men laughed and soon after, they docked at the long stone causeway on the far shore. The structure led up to the largest monuments in the world. Other small ships anchored and disembarked passengers who hoped to visit the pyramid.

Paru and his men approached the magnificent lion-shaped guardian of the complex. They stood motionless for a few moments, letting the glorious sight stir their Kas.

The sergeant said, "It never fails to amaze me."

Paru asked, "What? The Great Lion or the Pyramid?"

"The Pyramid, of course."

"Look to the left of it. You can see the foundation of Pharaoh Khafre's new pyramid."

Nafi turned to where he pointed. "Yes. Will he try to make his tomb bigger than his father's?"

Paru shook his head. "No one knows. The chamberlain says Pharaoh Khafre's will not be taller than his father's out of respect to his memory."

They left the causeway and walked through the sand a short distance to the paws of the Great Lion. Paru stopped. "The brigade will wait here while the sergeant and I go inside the temple."

"That's fine with us, Captain. This place gives me the shivers," one of the men said.

Paru raised his voice. "Stay sharp. Look for anyone or anything unusual or that is out of place."

He and Nafi took the steps leading down below the Great Lion and passed through the magnificent columns of the temple. The large sanctuary was cooler than outside, and lamps placed in front of each column provided the only light. A priest came to greet them.

"We've come to speak with Lord Roi," Paru said.

"I'm sorry, Captain. Haven't you heard? Our father, Lord Roi, sleeps now in the House of the Dead. They are preparing him for his eternal journey."

Paru's jaw dropped. He looked at the sergeant and then said, "My apologies. We're sorry to learn of this. How did he die?"

The priest pointed across the large underground chamber. "The granite statue of our Pharaoh fell on him, crushing him to death. But as you can see, Pharaoh Khafre is back in place. He is fine and there's not a scratch on him."

Paru scowled. "I can't believe what I am hearing. You put a strange value on life, holy one. Your priestly father is dead, and yet you can only think of Pharaoh's statue. Statues don't fall on their own."

"You're right, Captain. It took twenty men to stand it up again." The priest placed his palms together and smiled. "It is not just an image of Pharaoh, Captain. It represents his majesty's power and Ka. My concern for Lord Roi is over. Even as we speak, he begins his joyful journey into perfect Maat and the golden life that is to come."

There was something about the priest that Paru didn't like. He was about to leave, but stopped and asked, "Where did Prince Kasmut die, brother?"

"This way," the priest said. He led them to the back of the temple altar. "It happened while he was admiring the new paintings of Khufu's life that the assassin attacked."

He opened the door to a room perhaps fifty feet square containing a display of large paintings, and other art objects of the present Pharaoh's ancestors. Paru marveled at the colorful depictions of the great Khufu's victories and his building of the Great Pyramid.

"You mean he was in here alone? No one stayed with him?" Sergeant Nafi asked.

"The guards were here, outside in the temple sanctuary. He asked to be alone to contemplate the paintings."

"So he *was* alone," Paru said. "Gods! Anyone could have stabbed him."

The priest didn't respond, but turned and moved away a short distance. He scratched his bald head. "During that afternoon I did hear the high priest mention someone's name, Captain, if it would help."

"Yes?

"I believe it was Nubuti, Nebiti or 'Buti I think—or something like that."

The sergeant grumbled. "Captain. That's your servant's name."

Paru ignored the remark. He thanked the priest and walked quickly back onto the causeway and headed for their boat.

"Hurry men," the sergeant shouted to the brigade. "The captain's going to leave without us."

When Paru returned to the barracks, he asked for his horse and rode to the chamberlain's villa.

Hui came to the door. "Ah, Captain, you're back. Come in, my master isn't here. His chest was bothering him and he's gone to see his physician.

"It's good then, Hui. I've found out something serious and don't know how to handle it."

"Really? What is it?"

"It concerns my servant, Nubuti."

"'Buti? In what way?"

"I'm afraid he murdered the prince."

In the queen's apartment, mother and daughter sat drinking a cup of wine and enjoying honey cakes the princess loved.

"Why did the prince go to Giza, Mother? Why to the Great Lion guarding the Pyramid?"

The queen's face changed. She pursed her lips and closed her eyes for a moment, then took a deep breath. "The gods will punish me, Hettie. I should never have suggested the prince visit the new work done in the temple. How horrible for him to die like that."

"You could not have known, Mother. It is not your fault."

"Is it not?"

"What?" Her mother's face looked drawn and her eyes narrowed into something sinister. "Oh Mother, you could not have known someone would attack the prince."

"How can you be so sure, my child? I would not have allowed you to marry that beast. I would make sure Khafre did not give you to him."

Hettie suddenly became fully alert. For a moment she wasn't sure she knew the woman sitting next to her. Had the queen taken the dagger from her room and arranged Kasmut's death? Why would she put her own daughter in danger of Pharaoh's anger?

CHAPTER FOUR

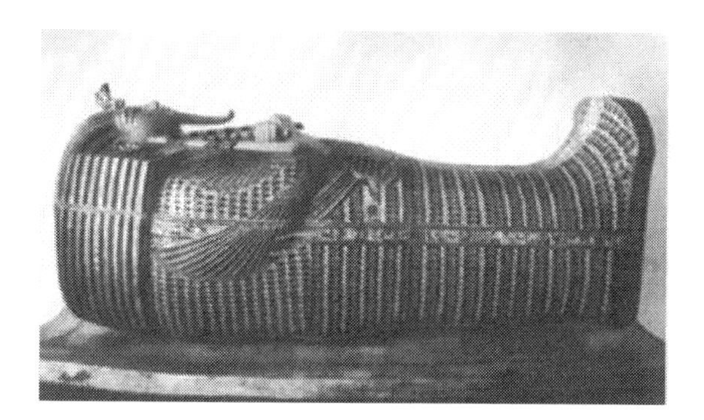

Hettie didn't know how to react to her mother's statements. If true, the queen had saved her from marrying the disgusting man. She also knew her father must never find out.

Her mother said, "You may know that many believe the Great Lion guarding the Pyramid is not a lion at all—but the god Anubis, the Jackal. Anubis guards the dead after all. But I agree with your father. It is a statue of a lion—the symbol of every Pharaoh's power. That is why Khafre is repairing the face." She stood, walked over and leaned on one of the columns supporting the roof of the veranda. "Put this tragedy behind you, Hettie. You will choose a husband one day. Make sure he is worthy."

Hettie would have liked to ask more, but the look in her mother's eyes changed her mind. She kissed her mother on the cheek and left the apartment.

Captain Paru threw Nubuti into the stockade when he learned what his servant had done. The dark cell reeked of human waste and Nubuti shifted nervously on the floor. To be awaiting Pharaoh's judgment was a dreadful thing. He would never see his family again. In the middle of the night, while he tossed and turned on the floor, the lock to his cell clinked and he jumped, surprised to find friends in the Guards there to break him out. The moon peered over the horizon as he headed for the river. Untying a fisherman's canoe, he paddled toward Giza on the other side. He would go to the temple and try to find out if his family back home was safe.

Inside the temple, he found a priest and approached him. "Holy one, is Roi the priest here? I need to speak with him."

"Roi? Ah, yes. I'll send someone to bring him."

"Thank you."

"You can wait in the gallery behind the altar if you wish."

Nubuti walked along the columns and entered the room. He began to sweat, clasped and unclasped his hands, pacing back and forth. What was taking so long? Finally, the priest returned.

"They couldn't find Roi, 'Buti. No one knows where he is."

Nubuti began to tremble. The priest knew his name. He shouldn't have come. Something wasn't right. "Thank you priest, I'll come back."

"I don't think so."The priest pulled a curved kopesh sword from under his robe and swung it at the young man.

Nubuti instinctively tried to protect his throat, but it was too late. Blood covered his hands and he couldn't cry out, only gurgled before everything went black.

Captain Paru should have suspected it. It had been two days since Sergeant Nafi told him of Nubuti's escape. The sergeant had ferreted out those responsible, and forced them to share Nubuti's cell until Paru decided their fate. He told the captain that his servant must have fled across the river to Giza. Paru sent Nafi across to see what he could find about his fugitive servant.

Nafti returned that evening. "You are not going to believe this, Sir. We found people who saw 'Buti waiting outside the temple. The priest, they said—you remember the one we met there—took Nubuti inside, but he didn't come out. We talked to one of the temple servants who said he and another worker had washed away a lot of blood in the exhibit room behind the altar."

"Blood?" Paru said. "'Buti's blood?"

"It must have been, Captain, although his body was not found. The servants said he vanished after that day. And here's something else. The priest has also disappeared. We met with an older priest who assured us he was in charge of the temple, but told us no priest matching our description served there."

"And so the mystery of the Great Lion grows." Paru rubbed his chin and stood. "Pharaoh must not learn of this, Nafi. It was my servant who was involved, and he will think I am behind it. But all these murders? Who is responsible?"

"My men will say nothing, Captain. I've ordered them not to share anything with their comrades. If anyone asks them why they went to Giza, they were to say they were following up on the death of Prince Kasmut."

"Good, well done."

Sergeant Nafi saluted and left.

Hui awoke the next morning, but quickly realized something was wrong. The house was too quiet. Iset wasn't on his bed and his adopted father was not puttering in the kitchen. He called to his cat.

Iset only mewled plaintively.

Leaping from his bed, Hui ran to Phanes' room and found him on the floor with Iset sitting beside him.

"Meowrrr?"

"Father," Hui shouted. He shook the older man's shoulders gently and then a little harder.

"Oh..." Phanes groaned. "My chest."

"Horus, help him!" Hui cried. "I'll be right back."

He ran to the front door and shouted to the guards assigned to protect the Chamberlain. "Hurry. Find a stretcher. It's my father."

When they rushed in a short time later, he helped them put Phanes on it. Leaving Iset in the house, he walked beside his father to the physician's dwelling.

People on the road moved out of the way and since the physician lived about a mile from them, they were there in good time.

The physician's servant told him that Lord Kebu was in the surgery. The guards followed Hui into the courtyard and he called out the physician's name.

Lord Kebu came out and when he saw Phanes, rushed to his side. "Inside quickly, men," he ordered. "Lift him onto the table, gently, gently." He grabbed Hui's arm. "What's wrong with him, Hui?"

"It's his chest, my Lord. He's been having pain."

The physician dismissed the guards and Hui sat down while the physician began his examination.

Phanes tried to speak but Kebu shook his head. "Hui, bring me a cup of wine. Tell the steward to hurry with it."

Hui nodded and rushed out. When he returned, Lord Kebu chose a powder from his medicines, poured some in the cup and stirred it before helping Phanes sit up a little to swallow it. "It will help with the pain, old friend." He turned to Hui. "Let's move him to the bed in the examining room. He'll be comfortable, and you can stay with him of course."

"Thank you, my Lord. I am grateful."

Lord Kebu stayed with his patient, checking his pulse and reassuring him.

When Phanes realized Hui was there, he reached out and took his hand. "Ah, Hui." He beckoned with his fingers for him to come closer. The thin, pale-faced man coughed and had difficulty speaking. "There is something I have never told you these many years. Listen carefully."

Hui leaned in so he could understand his mentor's words.

Phanes grimaced as pain struck him and he groaned. "I promised your mother I'd take her secret with me to my tomb. But as the gods have given me more breath, I believe they want me to tell you." He coughed again and paused a moment. "I've always told you that you were abandoned, but it is not so. Your mother was Princess Meresankh, youngest daughter of Pharaoh Khufu." He smiled before continuing. "Yes, my son—Khufu the Great. Your mother loved a soldier, but the king forbade their marriage. You were the fruit of their love, Hui. She died giving birth to you, and your father fell in battle a short time later. When neither family wanted you, I adopted you as my own."

Hui, overcome by what he had heard, could hardly speak. He pulled a chair closer and as his knees gave out, sat down. He took a deep breath and held on to Lord Phanes' hand. Royal blood? How was it possible? The gods must be playing a cruel trick on him. Khufu the Great was now his grandfather? It was preposterous. The old man must be delusional. No, it wasn't possible.

"Rest now, my Lord," he said. "Save your strength. What do I care for royal relations? You are my father and always have been. Please do not leave me."

Lord Phanes asked for more water. Hui held the cup for him and the frail old man sipped awhile before continuing.

"You must tell Queen Persenet your mother's name. Tell her it was I who told you. In the drawer by my bed is a document for you and a ring that belonged to your mother. Show it to her. The blood of the great Khufu flows in your veins, my dear Hui." He grimaced with pain again and then closed his eyes.

Hui stepped out of the small chamber. "Lord Kebu. Please come. Is he still breathing?"

The healer hurried in and took a small brass mirror and placed it under Phanes nostrils. He smiled as the moist mist of breath appeared on it. He looked up at Hui and nodded.

"Thank the gods," Hui said. "I'll stay with him as long as you allow, my Lord."

"Certainly. It will help him to know you are beside him."

As Hui sat watching the only family member he had ever known breathe in and out, his mind was so confused he had to close his eyes and concentrate on what Phanes had told him. The proof was at home in the drawer of his father's bedstead. How could he find the courage to tell Pharaoh? How would the royal family react to the arrival of an unknown relative? Did the royal family know about his mother having a child?

Lord Kebu came in from time to time to check on his patient and Hui stood by the open window. He was glad for the fresh air as opposed to the scent of medicines and herbs in the surgery. He could barely hear his father breathing and he had to put his head close to the old man to make sure he was still alive.

However, as the sun stood directly overhead, Lord Phanes breathed his last. Hui called for the physician to come in, and he confirmed that Phanes' Ka had left his old body and had begun its eternal journey.

"Let his name be remembered," the physician recited.

Tears filled Hui's eyes and his voice broke. "It will be so."

The physician nodded and said, "I will help you make his final arrangements."

"Thank you, my Lord. First, I must go home, and then his Majesty must be told."

He walked home and found Iset waiting for him at the door, crying as if she knew something had happened. She followed him into his father's bedchamber as he pulled out the drawer and found everything Phanes said would be there. He held up the ring to the sunlight and marveled at the engraving and flecks of gold on it. He slipped it into the pocket of his robe and examined the parchment legacy giving him everything. The official seal of the chamberlain's office bore Phanes imprint in the wax.

He put out some food for Iset. "I'm going to the palace, little one." He picked her up and put her on Phanes' bed so she could sense the old man's presence. She curled up and closed her eyes.

When Hui reached the palace that afternoon, the guards recognized him but wouldn't let him pass.

"Let me in. I must see his Majesty."

"I'm sorry, Hui," the guard said. "You cannot pass."

"Send for Captain Paru. He'll take me through."

The guard scowled. "We can't be bothered with you, shadow of Phanes. Be on your way."

Hui shouted at the top of his voice, "Paru. Come here!"

The soldiers became agitated and moved toward him. "Quiet. You're disturbing the palace."

"Paru," Hui shouted even louder, and the guards grabbed him.

"Let me go."

"What is it, Hui?" Captain Paru growled. "You know you can only pass when you're with the chamberlain. Bring him with you next time."

The guards released Hui and he brushed off his tunic. His throat was dry with the sadness he felt. "His Ka is no longer with us, my friend. I must tell his Majesty."

Paru's attitude changed immediately. "I'm sorry, Hui. Of course, follow me." At the large apartment doors, he opened one and called for Pharaoh's steward. The man nodded and went back inside.

Paru said to his friend, "I didn't give him the reason you have come. You must tell Pharaoh yourself."

"Thank you, Captain."

The door opened again, and the steward motioned for Hui to enter. Before he could make obeisance, Pharaoh raised his hand.

"Hui? Is this important? I am needed in the Audience Hall."

"Forgive me, Majesty, I understand." Hui had trouble controlling his emotions and tears threatened to fill his eyes. "I regret to inform you that my father is at this moment on his way to the House of the Dead."

Khafre's face contorted and became drawn. "Oh no." He touched his lips with the fingers of his right hand, and then touched his forehead. "We will remember his name forever."

"Even so," Hui recited

Pharaoh bowed his head for a moment, and then approached Hui. "Come with me, son. I loved the old man. Egypt has lost a great man and me, a good friend." He signaled to the steward, "Bring the queen." They walked into the front room and Khafre invited Hui to sit.

A few moments later, Lady Persenet entered and Pharaoh told her the sad news. She walked over to Hui and placed her hand on his shoulder. "We weep with you, my boy."

Hui's eyes filled with tears again. "I'm embarrassed, Majesty. I beg forgiveness."

"Nonsense," Queen Persenet said. "You were his son. Hettie has told me you thought of him as your father. We too will miss him." She moved from where he was sitting and spoke quietly with her husband before returning to him. "Come with me out on my veranda, Hui. Be at peace as you mourn your father."

"Go, my son," Khafre said. "When Phanes leaves the House of the Dead in seventy days, we will give him a glorious burial." Pharaoh then did the unthinkable. He put his arm across Hui's shoulders and led him toward the queen's apartment.

"Thank you, Majesty."

The queen took his arm and led him through her apartment and out onto the veranda. "Sit here." She clapped her hands and servants rushed to provide every comfort to her guest.

At that moment, Princess Hettie entered her mother's apartment. "Hui. What are you doing here? And you dare sit in my mother's presence?"

"Daughter, speak kindly. The gods have taken Hui's father."

Hettie's eyebrows raised, and then tears began to form. "Apologies, Hui. I did not know." She rushed over to him and sat on the arm of his chair, putting her arms around him. "I am so sorry." Her eyes showed only warmth and concern for him.

"Thank you, Highness. He loved you and your family very much."

Hettie rubbed her chin for a moment, something she always did when she was thinking. She stood and addressed her mother. "He cannot go home to the empty house, Mother. We can let him stay in Menkaure's old room."

"A thoughtful suggestion," Lady Persenet said. Do stay with us, Hui. Our older son, Menkaure's room is always ready for guests. As an officer in his father's army, he has not been home in two years."

"You are kind, Majesty. I only fear for Iset."

"Iset? Who is that?"

Hettie smiled and shook her head. "It is his cat, Mother. She is adorable. Let us bring her here by all means."

"If you think it is necessary," the queen said.

"I know how we can do it," Hettie said. "We will send Paru for her. Iset knows him and she will not be afraid."

"Tell him the door key is on the lintel," Hui said. "She's upset that Phanes didn't come home. The cat was attached to the dear man."

"I must leave the palace for a while, Hui. I am to accompany my brother. He is to award medals to the soldiers of the Third Army. When I return, we will share happy stories about your father."

"Thank you, Highness."

After Hettie left, the queen sat with him in the shade of a large palm. "What will you do now?"

"Well, when I looked in the drawer by my father's bed as he told me, I found my legacy. I inherit the villa and all his wealth. He was most generous."

As they talked, Hui was unsure about telling her what had been revealed to him by his dying father. He reached in the pocket of his tunic and rubbed the ring. She could have him arrested of course, and Pharaoh could have him executed, eliminating an unwanted heir in the royal family. He made a fist with his right hand and squeezed it as hard as he could several times, trying to work up the courage to speak.

Queen Persenet said, "It is good Lord Phanes trained you to be chamberlain. Pharaoh will be pleased you can step in."

"If he so wills it, my Lady."

"And a wife, Hui? You are still very young. How old are you?"

e seen twenty summers, Majesty. I will marry when I find the right one."

"Ah, a man who prefers to choose his wife rather than buy her."

"That's it, Majesty, of course." He paused for a moment to take a sip of wine to moisten his dry throat. "Majesty, I'm afraid to say what I have been told by my father to tell you." His hands were trembling and he took another sip of his drink.

"Oh?" the queen leaned toward him in her chair. "That sounds mysterious."

"It is, Majesty. I'm not sure I can believe it."

"Well, let me be the judge, Hui. Tell me what it is."

He nodded and began. "Lord Phanes said he was at my mother's side when I was born. She didn't survive the delivery and he adopted me because my father was a soldier and died in battle shortly after." Hui paused to think about how to say the rest. "He told me to tell you, Majesty, that her name was Meresankh."

The queen gasped, and dropped her drink. "No…it is not possible!"

CHAPTER FIVE

All color drained from the queen's face and she turned away. "This isn't possible, Hui. Your father must be wrong."

Hui reached into his pocket and took out the ring. "Here's proof, Majesty."

The queen's eyes widened as she took it from him. Examining it closely, she said, "This is definitely her cartouche."

"Are you all right, my Lady?"

Queen Persenet lowered herself onto a divan. Her hands trembled and she gazed out over the city below. Finally, she said, "Do you realize this means you have the royal blood of

Khufu in you? That makes you more important to Khafre than I am."

"Surely it isn't so, Majesty. I am a simple commoner. To be royal is to be of the gods. I am certainly not worthy of it."

She turned to him and smiled, waving her hand in a formal gesture. "Khafre will be very pleased. He will declare to the whole court that you are family. Your future with us is assured."

"Pharaoh may not want me at court, my Lady."

"No, Hui. Your mother was his sister—a princess, and not just any princess, but the daughter of the Great Khufu. Khafre worshiped his sister and his father. He will be very proud."

"I *would* like to stay," Hui said.

Lady Persenet nodded. "Well then, rest here on the veranda awhile until Hettie returns. She will have a lot to share with you about your adopted father. Let us remember his name." She touched the tips of her fingers to her lips and forehead.

"Even so," Hui recited.

She encouraged him to stretch out on the divan and then left. He closed his eyes and dozed until something soft tapped him on the cheek. He opened his eyes. "Iset, there you are." He picked her up and sat her on his lap.

Captain Paru walked onto the veranda. "At first Iset didn't want to leave the house. But she wasn't afraid of me and let me pick her up." He glanced around. "Why are you here in the queen's apartment?"

Hui pet Iset and she purred and pushed her head against his chest. "Pharaoh has invited me to stay here until things are resolved."

"Resolved?"

"I'll tell you later, my friend."

"Very well. Once again, I'm sorry your father is gone. I liked the old gentleman."

"Thank you."

When Paru turned, he found himself face to face with the princess. Making sure no one else was around, they embraced and kissed briefly.

"All right," Hui said. "Enough." He grinned as Paru scowled at him and left. To see another man kissing his love became unbearable and it was all he could do to keep quiet.

Walking out onto the veranda, Hettie pulled up a chair next to her friend and sat down. For a long time she shared her memories of his adopted father. How Phanes caught the both of them hiding in the secret passageway, listening in on ambassadors and other matters of the court. How more than once, the chamberlain ordered them tied to chairs so they wouldn't get into mischief. They were amusing stories of happy days and of a wonderful man.

Pharaoh called into the apartment. "Where is Hui?"

"I'm here, Majesty." Hui stood and walked back into the front room.

"Come sit with me. The queen has told me your story. I could not be more pleased."

"I'm glad, Majesty, the court is all I know. It's always been my second home."

"We have much to talk about," Pharaoh said.

The princess left them and Hui's eyes followed her as she headed for her mother's room. He knew she would be eager to know what it was all about.

"What did you say, Mother?" Hettie exclaimed. "I cannot believe it."

"He is Khufu's grandson. His mother was Princess Meresankh, and this is her ring." She showed it to her daughter.

"Seth's cursed breath!"

"Stop swearing, Hettie, you sound like your father. Do you know what Hui's heritage means? Not only has he become very wealthy but he is your cousin and part of our royal family. Do you understand?"

The princess stretched out on her mother's bed. "No, I'm not sure I do."

"Pharaoh will announce to the court that Hui is of royal blood. That means he will be eligible to marry any noble lady at court. Perhaps…even a princess."

The queen's words so startled Hettie, she sat up abruptly. "You cannot possibly be thinking of Hui for me, Mother. He is like a brother. It would be impossible."

Her mother stood and walked to the open window. A breeze filled the room with the fragrance of jasmine and she loved the colorful oleander blossoms. "Your father likes him. You don't want another Prince Kasmut in your future do you?"

"Of course not, but I beg you, please let me choose a husband for myself."

"Pharaoh cannot give you such a liberty, Daughter. Pharaoh always has the final word in these matters. Why do you think I had one of my attendants steal your dagger and bribe that horrible priest? I was hoping your father would come to his senses and pardon you once he understood how wrong Kasmut would be for you. You were never in real danger. Khafre would not have harmed you."

Hettie felt her face flush with anger. "You could not have been sure of that, Mother. I believe you were trying to get rid of me! I don't understand it." She turned to leave the room.

"Seth's naughty bits!" The queen swore and then flushed with embarrassment. "God's forgive me. Stay, Daughter. I was wrong for not telling you."

Hettie opened the door. "I need time to think on all this, Mother."

"Of course. But always remember, you are very precious to both of us."

The princess nodded, and left the apartment. She walked down the long corridor, her mind in a whirl.

"Meow..." Iset ran after her.

"There you are little one." Hettie stooped and picked her up. She smiled as the cat blinked at her with her large yellow-green eyes. "Listen to my plan, Iset. For now, I will pretend that Hui and I are interested in each other. My parents might leave me alone and Paru could continue to meet me at Hui's villa without suspicion. What do you think?" She continued down the corridor talking to the cat as if she were a friend.

"Arowwwow?"

"I know. It would not be fair to Hui, but I think he would still want to help me."

Iset suddenly became fidgety and jumped out of the princess's arms.

"Meowooowww..."

The princess turned and discovered Hui heading toward her. "Have you and Father finished then?"

Iset ran over to him and allowed him to pick her up.

"Yes, we have. He told me he would acknowledge me as his nephew before the court next week. I didn't know what to say. I have Pharaoh as my uncle."

She didn't answer immediately. When she did, her voice had softened. "I cannot believe we are cousins. This is all so wonderful." Taking his arm, they walked over to one of the alcoves and sat on a polished granite bench. The river below glistened in the sunlight and a tall palm sheltered them from the sun. "Tell me what you and he talked about." She listened as he told her about their discussion. She had never really noticed his eyes before. They were so large and had copper flecks in them like her own. She liked that he and she were the same height and when she had taken his arm, his bicep felt firm. She had been pleased when her body responded to his closeness.

When Hui picked up the cat, she jumped onto Hui's shoulder and flicked her tail back and forth between them.

"Stop that, Iset," Hui said.

Hettie laughed. "She is jealous. Look at her."

Hui nodded and stood. "I must be going, Highness. I didn't sleep well last night. We'll talk again."

Hettie smiled at him. "Rest well, Cousin."

He returned her smile. "I'm just an old owl, remember?" He turned and headed toward her older brother's room.

The next morning, Hui opened his eyes to find Iset staring at him. She swatted his tousled hair with her paw.

"All right, Lady," he said. He grabbed her and she let out a feline squeak. Hui laughed and climbed out of bed. It was hard for him to believe he had actually slept in the palace.

A servant entered. "Good morning, my Lord. Your bath awaits."

"Oh? Where do I go?"

"It's on the porch outside your room, my Lord. You may undress there."

One did not thank servants for doing what was expected. He nodded and opened the door to the outside. Iset followed at his heels. Taking off his clothes, he sank down into the warm water. "Ah," he sighed as he inhaled the pleasant scent added to the water.

Iset jumped onto a small wooden bench next to the copper bath and sniffed the air. She made funny faces, sneezed and sputtered at the smell of the perfumes and spices.

A familiar voice said, "Good morning, Hui."

Startled by the intrusion, Hui said, "Prince Duaenre. It is good to see you."

Iset jumped from the bench and walked over and rubbed against the crown prince's shins.

"Who is this?"

"It's Iset, Highness. The most spoiled cat in the land."

The prince laughed. "May I pick her up?"

"Of course. That's what she wants."

Dua bent down, lifted her carefully and sat with her on the bench next to Hui's tub. His princely braid on the right side of his head fascinated the cat. She began batting it with her paw, making it swing back and forth.

"Remember to tell the servants to shave you," Dua said.

"Must I, Highness? Shaving my face is fine, but not the body."

"If you are part of the royal family, it is expected. You must act and dress accordingly."

"Hettie sent you to pester me, didn't she? She loves torturing me."

Dua's laugh was more of a snort. "I do not take orders from a mere princess, Hui. No one orders the crown prince except Pharaoh." Then he grinned. "Don't worry. They do not have to shave you every day."

"Well, that's a relief."

Dua laughed and the cat jumped down and chased after an intruding grasshopper. The prince stood. "I will meet you at the dining table when you are done."

"Agreed."

Iset walked along the edge of the tub and whispered, "Meoarrr..."

"I agree," Hui said. "I like him too."

Attendants returned with pumice stones and copper razors to rid his body of unwanted hair. He was not looking forward to this practice if was to be done daily.

After dressing, Hui made his way to the king's dining room. The prince and princess were there and he fell immediately face down on the floor when he discovered Pharaoh Khafre sitting at the head of the table.

"Stand, Nephew," Pharaoh said. "No need for ceremony in our home."

"Thank you, Majesty." Hui sat next to Dua and a servant brought him a plate of soft-boiled eggs, a slice of watermelon and a still-warm loaf of bread. A clay pot of fresh honey sat in the center of the table.

No one spoke as they ate, and Hui felt self-conscious. He was certain Hettie was paying too much attention to the way he ate, which only made him more nervous.

"Meoww…" the cat said.

"What is that sound?" Pharaoh asked.

"I'm sorry, Majesty. She must have followed me. May I present Iset, my cat and confidant?

Pharaoh patted his knee. "Come," he said.

Iset couldn't resist. She purred and jumped onto the lap of the ruler of the world. He stroked her head causing her to purr even louder.

Khafre smiled. "Iset is it? She's another servant of our mother goddess."

"Oh, and she is very wise, Father," Hettie said.

Hui smiled watching his cat and the king. Iset now had Pharaoh in her power.

Khafre pushed his chair back. "Today Hui, I will reveal to the court your true identity." He paused a moment. "I deeply loved Meresankh. My sister had a mind of her own, much like Hettie. We never knew she had a child or had fallen in love with that soldier, hmm, what was his name? Alim, that was it. Yes, Captain Alim. We knew she was interested in him, but when Alim was killed, she ran off and disappeared. Our parents kept if from us. We only knew she had died from some illness when her sarcophagus arrived from Abydos. It was a sad time for us all."

Hui didn't know what to say. "You said, 'Captain Alim,' my Lord. Doesn't his name mean 'wise one?"

Pharaoh nodded. "Appropriate, isn't it? To be the son of *two* wise men?"

Hui smiled. "Thank you, Majesty. It is a kind thought."

Pharaoh pulled on his goatee for a moment. "I am naming you my new chamberlain. I know it may be awkward for you at first—but Lord Phanes—may we remember his name—trained you well."

Hui said, "We remember his name."

Pharaoh nodded. "It pleases me to give you his position."

"One cannot refuse Pharaoh," Hui answered. "I will accept the post to honor Phanes name."

"Good. Well said."

"Meowwrr…"

Khafre grinned. "Well, Iset agrees with me so that settles it."

Everyone laughed.

Captain Paru escorted Hui to the dressing room adjacent to the Audience Hall. "I'll leave you to get ready, Lord Chamberlain," he said.

"Stay, my friend. I feel awkward. My father's life has ended, and mine at court is only beginning, and I am not looking forward to the change. As chamberlain, I will need a friend."

Paru patted him on the shoulder. "You *have* a friend. I wish you well in court today, Hui. Some of these fat old courtiers can be as vicious as jackals. Don't let them get to you." He sat on one of the chairs in the small room.

Hui smiled, removed his tunic and placed it over a chair. He took his father's beautifully embroidered robe and allowed the attendant to place it over his head. It reached to the floor and was heavier than it appeared. "I don't know if I can walk in this thing," he groaned. He raised and lowered his arms to see if he could move them.

He said, "You know, what you said about the old courtiers made me smile. When I would come here with Father, he taught me that if I pictured them all as animals it would make me smile. Some actually resemble hippos, others perhaps a stork or fat frog. That's what I'll do today—thank you for the reminder. It's as if my father is here with me."

Paru chuckled. "Dare I ask what animal you see when you look at me?"

"A lion of course, Captain, just like your name."

"Ha! Yes, but with all the murders under the Great Lion at Giza, I've had enough with lions this week."

"Indeed. Three deaths, and are they connected?"

"Wait a moment, three? There were only two murders."

"No, my friend. You forgot to include the murder of the senior priest. Fifteen foot statues do not just fall on people."

"You are right, of course. I had forgotten, my Lord."

Hui frowned. "Don't make me nervous. I'm not a Lord yet."

One of the court scribes came to the door. "They're ready, Lord Chamberlain."

Paru waited by the door. Hui shrugged, resigned to his doom as he followed the scribe out into the Audience Hall, doing his best not to trip over the long robe.

That evening, the new chamberlain joined the royals for supper. After the simple meal, he sat with them in the living room. In a small alcove, a musician played a lute softly. Queen Persenet took an azure blue thread and with her needle, added the color to the embroidered river scene of fish and flying ducks.

Hui walked closer to examine her work. "It's beautiful, Majesty."

The cat followed him and tried to catch a thread with her paw before the queen rolled it up.

"I have been working on this pillow cover for two summers, young man. I only work on it when I'm unsettled."

Pharaoh grumbled. "Yes, and when she brings it out, it unsettles us all!"

Hettie and Dua laughed. "It is true," the prince said.

"Come play Hounds and Jackals with me, Lord Chamberlain," Pharaoh said, more of an order than a request.

"With pleasure, Majesty. But you should know I beat Lord Phanes all the time."

"Take care, Hui," Dua said. "Father does not always play by the rules."

"Throw that child in the river," Khafre shouted, and his children groaned in response.

The cat disappeared for a while but then Hui spotted her curled up on one of the divans near the musician. Her eyes were closed, mesmerized by the music.

As he and Pharaoh played, Khafre said, "I have decided to go to Giza and see for myself what is happening over there. You will accompany me in two days. I want to examine the progress on the Funerary Temple honoring my father—and as the gods have wonderfully revealed, *your* grandfather. The architect has also promised a tour inside the construction of my own pyramid."

"As you will, Great One. I love the monuments."

Khafre stopped smiling. "Yes, well, my brother Djedefre's pyramid was never finished. We have yet to decide what to do with it."

"Even so, Majesty, our beloved Egypt will remember you and your father for what you have built on the plateau."

His words pleased the king and he smiled. "Now let us talk about court today. What did you think of old Lord Titia?"

Hui chuckled. "He's a big bag of wind, Majesty. Did he actually say anything we could understand?"

Pharaoh guffawed. "Bag of wind! I like that. I will have to add that to my pet names for him."

Prince Dua overheard. He and his sister were playing cards close by. "It does not beat my favorite expression of yours, Father. You often say someone is as mad as a bag of frogs!"

Hettie giggled. "It is mine too."

"Please go on, Hui," the king said.

"I told Captain Paru this morning that I like to picture each person as an animal. When I face Lord Titia, I see a noisy old crow. Can't you picture it? Have you ever watched how he moves?"

Pharaoh chuckled.

"Then there's General Mahu," Hui said. "He resembles one of those giant poisonous toads. He has the same wide mouth and beady eyes. In addition, all of those large warts covering his face make me shiver when I look at him."

Hettie laughed. "I will never be able to keep a straight face when I meet him again."

Hui said, "I could go on Majesty, but it does help me get through the many debates in court. Over the years Lord Phanes let me watch, and you have to admit your advisors can be a bit stuffy at times."

Pharaoh smiled, and cleared his throat. "Yes, now tell me. How do you see me?"

The queen grinned. "Be careful, Hui."

"Oh, that's easy, Great One. I don't have to think about it at all. You are the falcon. Your sharp eyes closely examine everyone who comes before you. I've watched you pounce when they let their guard down. You are Horus, Majesty—without a doubt."

The family clapped for Hui when he finished and was glad to see the pleased expression on Khafre's face.

Pharaoh remained silent a moment, reached down and moved his last jackal piece of the game. "I win. You are wise for your age, Hui, but as the falcon, I can see your every move."

"And I can only be grateful, Lord Pharaoh."

The applause awakened the cat, and she stretched her long back and pranced toward Hui, who by now felt remarkably relaxed with Pharaoh's family. He glanced at Hettie, and she smiled. He remembered the touch of her arm on his as they walked together. Dare he hope she might see him as more than a friend?

The queen stood and left her embroidery on the chair. "I will say goodnight children." She turned toward Hui. "And that includes you, Lord Chamberlain."

"Thank you and good night, Majesty."

"Good night, Hui. Rest well," Pharaoh said, joining her.

The crown prince followed them, leaving Hui and the princess in the living room.

The musician departed leaving only the song of a nightingale in the distance. A soft whisper of the wind blew the curtains like the sails on Pharaoh's galley, filling the room with sweet fragrances from the garden.

"I love it here," Hui said. "Your parents have made me feel like part of the family."

"It is because we have known you all your life," she said. "It seems natural to have you with us."

He paused to think whether he should say what he was about to say. "I'm sorry I'm not your Captain Paru, my Lady. I know he would give anything to be in my place."

"You are just being kind, Hui. And I appreciate your words, but do not be too hard on yourself, *little owl*!"

Hui laughed.

"You see. I remember. You always acted wise and thoughtful like an old owl." She smiled and said in a more quiet voice, "You will make someone very happy one day."

"If she is like you, Hettie *the Ibis*, I would be happy indeed."

She giggled. "You haven't called me that in years."

"I know, and I always thought you were as beautiful and as gracious as the sacred bird—even though it is not an image worthy of you."

"Not so. I love the Ibis." She stood, wished him goodnight and was about to leave the room when she stopped. "I am glad you are here with us."

"Thank you, Princess. Good night."

Two days later, after sunup, His Majesty's royal galley, the *Eye of Horus* prepared to sail. High on the mast, long narrow thirty-foot banners flew in the wind, waving their royal colors of blue and yellow to the crowd on the dock below. Fifty oarsmen on each side of the ship waited with their oars held straight up. The crown prince and the princess were already on board.

"When do we sail, Hui?" Hettie asked. "Oh, I'm sorry, my *Lord Chamberlain*."

Hui laughed. "All right, if you don't stop, I'll use your official name all the time."

"Peace," Prince Duaenre said. "How does it feel to be one of us, Cousin?"

"No different, Highness, except I have to shave more often."

Hettie laughed.

A loud blast from the trumpets announced the arrival of Pharaoh. Khafre drove his chariot, pulled by a pair of magnificent white stallions. He looked more like a god than a man. On his broad, high forehead, he wore a tight-fitting blue crown. Beneath full, arched brows, his eyes darted like a falcon's. His nose was straight, his ears round and delicate, his chin strong and full. He was the image of power and strength.

He reigned in his horses at the gangway and stepped from his chariot onto a woven blue carpet. The instant his foot touched it, thousands of people fell prostrate before him, holding their palms toward the living god. Each warrior and crewman knelt on one knee and held his fist against his heart.

The Lord Chamberlain moved onto the gangway, held his staff high and shouted in his loudest voice: "People of Memphis. Bid farewell to the living Son of Ra."

Pharaoh raised his hand and the people stood and cheered. They clapped in a cadence used only for the king. It grew louder as more people pushed closer to the ship. Khafre turned and walked up the carpeted gangway. Trumpets sounded again and his majesty turned to face the crowd. Princess Hettie walked over and stood on his left. Her brother joined them on the right.

"May we have the order to depart, Majesty?" Hui asked.

"Set sail!" Pharaoh commanded.

CHAPTER SIX

It was a glorious sun-filled day on the river. The ship's captain signaled the crew to pull up the four anchors and unfurl the great rectangular sail. Three rudder-men took their posts and guided the *Eye of Horus* away from the dock. The wind caught the sail which bore a decorated eye of the god on it, giving the vessel the aspect of a creature coming to life. Pharaoh's galley slowly sailed south toward the Giza plateau. Hui inhaled the sweet smell of water hyacinths as the rainbow-hued wings of dragonflies flitted around the ship bidding it a pleasant journey. It would take two days to reach Giza and the great monuments.

He walked astern to admire the glorious city of Memphis growing smaller behind them.

Captain Paru ambled over and stood beside him. "Beautiful sight, isn't it?"

"Yes, my friend. Isn't this preferable to crossing in a felucca?"

Paru laughed. "Agreed."

They marveled as Pharaoh's galley pushed against the mighty current. Even with the sail, one hundred oarsmen and three at the rudders strained to keep the ship on course.

Pharaoh and his family strode up the steps to the royal deck and seated themselves on comfortable divans with plush striped cushions. The four—Pharaoh, the princess, the crown prince, and chamberlain—relaxed while servants tended to their needs and desires. They soon enjoyed wine and pastries. Tall men with large ostrich-feathered fans stood nearby to maintain a pleasant breeze and keep insects away.

At sun-up on the morning of the next day, the ancient shadow of the first pyramid at Saqqara poked up through the morning mist like a mountain—its six gigantic levels clearly identifiable. Hui brought a woven reed basket with a lid to carry Iset. He feared she might fall overboard and the basket had plenty of spaces for her to observe everything around her.

Princess Hettie had warned Hui to remain on deck with Captain Paru. She could then spend time with the handsome officer without arousing her father's suspicions.

The mid-day meal provided plenty of fresh broiled fish, bread, cheese, fruit and wine. The hot afternoon was for napping, or enjoying the spectacle of the countryside sailing past. Hui preferred the latter. He held Iset on his lap and she hissed at the hippos who snorted and opened their large jaws at the ship moving through them. At sunset, Pharaoh's galley anchored south of Giza, far enough away from land to avoid insects.

Early on the morning of the second day, Hui walked to the bow as the crew raised the anchors, and oarsmen—fifty on each side—lowered their oars into the water in rhythm. He raised his hand to shield his eyes to make sure the musicians were on the causeway to welcome the royal party. Long rows of priests awaited the king's arrival and crowds began to cheer as the galley approached.

Pharaoh stood with his hands on his hips. "I love to look at my father's pyramid from the river."

"As do I, Majesty. I hope to live long enough to see your pyramid join the great Khufu's."

Khafre scowled at him. "Forgive me, Hui, but by then I will have left this life. Please allow me more time before I join my ancestors in the life to come."

Hui grinned. "A thousand apologies, Majesty. May you live forever."

Pharaoh nodded and then laughed. "I will. Now, is everything ready?"

“Yes, King Who Will Live Forever. Tonight, when you return, the ship’s captain will move us away from shore to insure we enjoy a peaceful sleep.”

“Good. I sleep better on the ship. It must be the movement of the water.”

The chamberlain nodded.

Pharaoh walked over and peered into Iset’s carrying basket. “How is she taking to the ship?”

“She’s finally used to it, Majesty. I couldn’t have her falling overboard.”

“Agreed. Guard her well, Nephew. She is Pharaoh’s cat, too.”

“Yes, Great Eye of Horus. She adopted you very quickly.”

Pharaoh’s smile slid into a grin as he walked back to his cabin.

Pharaoh’s safety was Captain Paru’s primary concern on these voyages. While his countrymen knew they would die if they touched the royal person, there were still those who would risk eternal damnation to do him harm. The recorded histories of such assassinations were many, and for this visit, Paru requested two extra divisions of the regular army to guard the streets and monuments. Golden carrying chairs would transport the prince and princess as well as the chamberlain. Their bearers would be guardsmen instead of Nubian slaves. Pharaoh would disembark last.

Paru stood by his sergeant. "Thank the gods there are no tall buildings for assassins to fire arrows from. Of course, we must patrol the monuments, but I feel good about security."

"It is now in the hands of the gods," sergeant Nafi said.

Upon docking, Paru and his men went ashore first to get into position. Lord Hui followed and signaled for the bearers to bring the chairs. Pharaoh's visit would begin at the Funerary Temple of the Great Lion.

Hui told Pharaoh the order of the procession. "The priests of Horus and Ra will take their places at the front of the procession behind the orchestra which will lead the way. Princess Hettie will follow, then her brother, and finally you, Majesty, the most important of all. You will sit on the ivory and ebony throne on top of a thin, flat platform carried by fifty warriors."

"Very good. Proceed," Khafre said.

Hui gave the signal for the musicians to begin. His carrying chair would follow behind the king just in front of the five-hundred soldiers who had been standing at attention. When the music began, Hui sighed with relief.

"I heard that sigh, Hui," Pharaoh called to him over his shoulder. "You've done a good job."

"Thank you, Great Eye Who Sees All, or should it be the Great Ear?"

Pharaoh laughed and raised his hand to greet the people pressing forward to see him.

The chanting of the priests grew louder. Hui enjoyed their deep voices singing a melody that was triumphant and uplifting. It sounded like what he imaged the singing of the gods and goddesses in the afterlife might be like. Ahead, the Great Lion awaited, stretched out—its enormous paws welcoming the procession.

As they approached the monuments, Hui gasped. The head of the lion, now covered with wooden scaffolding, provided access to the sculptors repairing the great face. The likeness had changed. “It’s Khafre,” he said in surprise.

The procession came to a halt and soldiers helped move the crowd out of the way. His majesty would enter the temple he had designed. It stood below the base of the Great Lion, guarding the pyramid of his father.

The portable platform was lowered slowly and when his majesty stood, the people shouted his name—“Kha-fray! Kha-fray!”—louder and louder. He smiled and raised his hands in acknowledgment.

The bearers lowered Hui’s chair to the ground. He stepped out and prepared to walk behind the king, smiling at those closest to him.

“Come, Hui. It is an honor to be with the king.”

“Yes, Majesty, it is.”

“Walk beside me, my friend.”

A movement high up on the head of the Lion caught Hui's eye. Without warning, something struck him in the chest with such force it knocked him backward and he cried out in pain.

Pharaoh shouted Hui's name just as the young man collapsed into his arms.

A voice repeated his name over and over. Hui recognized the voice and opened his eyes. He grimaced and cried out in pain again.

"Easy," Pharaoh said. "Thank the gods you are alive. I knew a good man like you could not die."

Hui realized he was lying down in what must be the temple.

"Drink this, my Lord," the king's physician ordered. "Drink all of it to ease your pain."

Having been given the drug on the battlefield, Hui knew to hold his nose, and swallowed it down and then tried to sit up and look at his wound.

"Lie still," Pharaoh ordered. "You'll tear your bandages."

"What happened, Majesty?"

"You were struck by an arrow, Hui, and by Seth's foul stench, it was meant for me. Paru's men are in pursuit of whoever did it."

"I saw where it came from, Majesty. Someone was up on the head of the Lion in all that scaffolding."

Khafre growled. "We'll find him. The message wrapped around the arrow gives us a clue."

"Message?"

"Yes, it said, 'Djedfre lives.'"

"What?" Hui asked. "But Majesty, your brother's Ka is with the gods. What does the message mean?"

"Rest now. Let me worry about it. My physician will go with you to the ship."

Hui gritted his teeth as another surge of pain gripped him. He closed his eyes and prayed for the medicine to take effect. He opened them when his bearers lifted the makeshift stretcher and carried him out of the temple, down the causeway and up to his cabin.

Khafre's steward came inside and helped him into bed. "Such a horrible thing, my Lord."

"I know. They could have killed Pharaoh."

The servant made the sign against the evil eye. "I'll bring you some wine."

Hui let out a long sigh. "Please bring me beer instead."

The servant's face lit up. "Of course, sir. There's plenty cooling over the side." He left again and Hui ran his fingers over the bandage wrapped tightly around his chest. He touched a moist spot and found blood on his fingers.

The door opened again, but it was Lord Bata, the Physician. He pulled up a chair next to the bed and held Hui's wrist.

"Hmm. Your pulse is good. It's not as fast as before. Has the powder of the red flower helped at all?"

"Yes, it has, my Lord. Will you tell me what damage the arrow has done to my chest?"

"Horus protected you, my son. It struck mostly muscle for which you should be grateful. A rib deflected it away from your heart, bless the gods!"

"Bless Horus," Hui whispered

"It will take the wound the cycle of one moon to close up. You must do everything I prescribe. The stitches will allow for swelling to occur—it is only natural." He paused a moment. "In a way, I must thank you, my Lord."

"Oh? Why is that?"

"If the arrow had killed his Majesty I would have died. You know the law, if Pharaoh dies, so do I."

Hui nodded. "I am relieved his majesty is unharmed."

"Lord Chamberlain," a woman's voice called. The cabin door opened and the princess entered. The physician bowed to her and stepped outside.

"I'm sorry I am unable to get up, Highness," Hui said.

"What a stupid thing to say, Hui. No one expects you to get up. Gods! Men are hopeless."

"Not all men, my Lady. Is Paru hopeless?"

Hettie grinned. "No, definitely not. Now let me look at you." She pulled back the sheet and examined his large bandages more closely. "Bata does a good job."

Hui grabbed the sheet back and covered himself. "I don't know if he does, Princess. I can't see the stitches very well." He felt a pleasant warmth having her so close to him. The fragrance of her perfume was strong and he thought her eyes sparkled with fire.

"Why are you looking at me like that?"

"Don't chastise me for staring, Hettie. I might never have seen your face again. Allow me time to enjoy it."

She smiled. "My dearest orphaned owl. You say the nicest things."

Hui laughed. "I'm not an orphan. I have Pharaoh as an uncle, and two cousins—and don't forget Iset." He suddenly remembered his cat. "Seth's bowels!" he swore. "Hettie, will you find her for me? She must be worried, the poor little thing."

"Of course. I just came to say that we're going to have the best time while you recuperate. I'll read to you and wait on your every wish. I will spoil you like you spoil Iset." She laughed, got up and left the cabin.

"Horus help me." Hui sighed, waiting for the beating of his heart to return to normal.

The physician returned and Hui thought he'd better warn him. "The princess has decided to be my nurse, my Lord. You've got to protect me."

Bata smiled. "Shame on you, Hui. Think how many men would gladly take an arrow if they knew the princess would take care of them." Hui made a face and the physician said, "All right, I'll make sure she doesn't overdo it."

"I'm grateful."

The rest of the day passed slowly. Hui was aware that Pharaoh returned and departed again. Hettie explained that he was going to examine the work on his pyramid. Construction placed his to the left of his father's. Finally, Hui fell into a deep sleep and awoke to find Iset purring near his head.

"Meow…owlll . ." she patted his forehead before he drifted off again.

CHAPTER SEVEN

Hui grew stronger every day. His cat, unhappy he spent so much time in bed, whined and refused to let him pet her, hiding under the bed in protest. Giving in, he put her on his shoulder and walked her around the garden twice a day. They were back living in his father's house instead of the palace. He preferred it to the royal residence because it held fond memories for him. When the royal family returned to Memphis, he insisted they allow him to move back home.

Iset loved re-discovering her secret hiding places with the smells and skittering creatures she liked to chase.

Lord Ameni, Pharaoh's physician, came every day to change his bandages, and recite prayers for healing to the gods. He was pleased that after only three weeks Hui didn't need the pain or sleeping powders. He could stand and move about easily but was careful not to overdo things.

"Your scar is forming nicely, my friend," Ameni said. "You can show it with pride to the young women at court."

"It still hurts if I stretch my right arm and shoulder."

"When you are well enough, Highness, we will exercise it."

A week later, while Hui was sunning himself on the veranda, and reading dispatches from the king, Hettie arrived with four strangers—all female.

"I've brought these women for you, Hui. You can select a housekeeper from them."

"Ah—can I? It is kind of you to allow me to choose for myself." His sarcastic tone let her know he was not pleased.

In the end, after several hours of watching the women work and sampling their cooking, Hui chose Kebi. He walked into the front room and Hettie followed him.

"Kebi prepares fish and poultry the way I like them," he explained. "And I like her name—it refers to the busy bee, and she certainly likes to keep herself occupied." He didn't add that he found her attractive and that she reminded him of the princess. Her curvaceous figure added to her appeal and her complexion was the color of honey. She wore her hair short with bangs, and her eyes were deep green.

"Does Iset like her?" Hettie asked.

Hui smiled. "Iset took to her immediately, and Kebi will spoil her even more."

"Good, then I am glad I found someone to look after you." She sat down beside the cat who slept on the divan. "You are still going to bring Iset to the palace aren't you? Father misses her already."

"Really? Of course, Highness, she does like that old place. You have so many secret rooms and passageways."

He couldn't help being attracted to Pharaoh's daughter, but he didn't know if he could continue to torture himself by allowing her to meet Paru in his house. When she was near, his pulse quickened. She refused to wear a wig as most courtiers did but kept her hair short and held together with a narrow circlet of gold. Her light skin resembled alabaster, a sure sign her ancestors were from Thinis in Southern Egypt. He purposely avoided her gaze, because her eyes made him nervous—as if they could see deep inside him.

There was a knock at the door and Kebi opened it, admitting Captain Paru.

"I don't want to intrude," he said. "I've brought more of his majesty's dispatches for you to read, my friend." He handed Hui a leather pouch and turned to face the princess.

Hui noticed Hettie's face flush as she stood.

"I was just going," she said. "But if you ask me nicely, I might sit with you on the veranda a while."

Kebi headed for the kitchen, and Captain Paru motioned with his head for Hui to leave.

"I have a better idea," Hui said. "Iset and I will go out on the veranda. You two stay here."

"Thank you," Hettie said.

Hui carried the king's dispatches with him and sat down on a wooden bench. Iset tip-toed after him. He bent over, picked her up and set her on his lap. Rubbing behind her ears, she rolled over so he could tickle her stomach. As content as he was with the cat, he envied Paru sitting now in the living room with the princess. How could he compete with the handsome warrior? The man possessed everything women like—strength, bravery and good looks. Hui didn't stand a chance.

Opening the royal dispatches, he read through the first letter and was surprised to learn there had been a witness to the attack. The man had seen the archer and given a description of him. Tall, thin, and he bore a blue birthmark on his bald head. At first, Hui thought the information might prove helpful, but to narrow it down to where the attacker came from would be difficult.

The second dispatch was a report from the Army of the South. There had been an incursion of Nubian warriors across the border and an attack made at the Egyptian fort at Abu—the island of elephants. Hui's father had told him many times that the Nubians were ancient enemies. The southern army would have to act quickly to stop another invasion. Several other messages dealt with the expansion of Egypt's fortress at Kadesh in the north. There was also the appointment of a new governor to the Nome at Awen.

"We're leaving," Paru called to him from inside.

"Not together, please," Hui called back.

"No, I'm leaving first," Hettie said. "My bearers are waiting."

"Thank you for coming, Princess," Hui said. "Iset loves your visits." He didn't know what else to say. It was he who looked forward to them. Her being in his house was like water from the sacred river inundating the parched earth. She brought life to it.

Hettie bowed her head to him and left.

Hui said, "Will you call Ranofer for me, Paru? I want to dictate responses to the king's dispatches."

"Of course." Paru walked down the hall and returned with the young scribe who sat at the writing desk and prepared his pen.

Paru said, "I'll be going. Hettie and I treasure this place. If only. . ."

"Yes, I know. I have plenty of '*if onlys*' in my life too. Thank you for bringing the dispatches."

"Very well." Paru nodded and left.

In the palace council chamber, the king's advisors talked among themselves waiting for his majesty to join them. As chamberlain, he would have a powerful voice in advising his majesty. He only prayed the wisdom of his father's training would be enough.

The great cedar doors opened and Pharaoh Khafre strode into the chamber. He personified a pharaoh—tall, powerfully built, smooth shaved head, his body adorned with golden necklaces and arm bands. By special dispensation, members of the council did not prostrate themselves in Khafre's presence. Instead, they acknowledged him by bowing their heads politely.

As Pharaoh took his place at the head of the table, he waved his hand permitting them to join him around it. Hui sat to his right.

Pharaoh said, "My Lords, I have also asked Captain Paru of the Guards to join us."

He nodded to Hui, who stood and walked toward the door. A guard opened it and Hui walked into the hall and motioned for the captain to enter. He whispered, "Be careful what you say. Speak only when spoken to."

"I know the protocol, Hui," Paru grumbled.

They entered the chamber and Hui regained his seat. Paru stood at attention.

"Be at ease, Captain," Pharaoh said. "You may sit at the end of the table."

"Thank you, Great One." He walked around and took his place.

Pharaoh studied his councilors for a moment before speaking.

Hui glanced around at each man. Most of them had been the king's father's trusted advisers and were old enough to remember him as a young prince.

Pharaoh said, "We wish to welcome Lord Hui to our council. His revered father—we remember his name—has trained him well. As my long lost nephew, Hui is more than chamberlain—he is family. Welcome Lord Chamberlain."

"Thank you, Divine Majesty. May I serve you as well as my father. His name is remembered."

"Even so," everyone recited.

"Now, Captain Paru," Pharaoh continued, "tell us what you have discovered about the failed attempt on our life."

The officer nervously cleared his throat. "We have a description of the assassin, Majesty, but that is all."

"Go on."

"He is tall and of a thin build. He also has a blue birthmark on his shaved or bald head. We have no other description of him."

Hui asked, "What about the senior sculptor of those working on the Great Lion's face, Captain? Anything from him?"

"He told me none of the sculptors were up there at that moment, my Lord. They had all climbed down and were trying to get closer to see his majesty."

"I see," Hui said. He turned toward one of the generals. "General Haka. Did your men block all ships and small boats trying to leave Giza?"

Pharaoh smiled at Hui like a parent pleased with a son's clever question.

"Yes, Lord Chamberlain. He could not have left Giza. They found no one matching the description. My men examined everyone, on my word of honor."

"Thank you, General, but that's not quite true is it?" Hui said.

The warrior shot back. "What do you mean?"

"You said no one could have left the plateau. But they could escape into the desert red lands, couldn't they?"

"The desert, of course, Hui," Pharaoh said.

"Yes, Majesty. Perhaps if he went that way, it's not too late to send a brigade to try and follow this man with the blue mark. I would very much like to go with them."

Pharaoh shook his head. "You? Out of the question. Your wound has not yet healed. We will not allow it."

"Then let me go, Majesty," Paru said.

Pharaoh Khafre frowned. "No, as Captain of the Guards, your place is here."

Paru then did something that made the councilors gasp. He stood. "Please, Great Pharaoh. I was responsible for your safety at Giza and failed. Let me redeem myself."

Hui motioned for Paru to sit down, but the officer didn't move.

Frustrated, and fearful for his friend, Hui raised his voice. "Captain, no one's head can be higher than the king's. Sit down."

The officer quickly did so. "Forgive me. I meant no disrespect."

Pharaoh nodded. "Your heart spoke before your head. You are only concerned for our safety and we are grateful. After consideration, we will give you the task of tracking down this man. May Horus go with you."

The king's councilors nodded in agreement.

"The army also failed you, Majesty," General Haka said.

"Then choose your best trackers to go with Paru."

"Thank you, Majesty," Haka's lips spread into a wide smile.

Khafre chose to change the subject. "Now we will discuss the dangerous situation in the south at Abu."

The council planned what action the army should take at the island as well as the fortress at Kadesh on the Asian border near the Negev Desert. By mid-morning, they adjourned and Pharaoh left the chamber. Several members congratulated Hui for surviving his first council.

Everyone left except General Haka. "My Lord, you sounded so much like your father today. It is good to have you with us."

"Kind words, General, thank you."

Haka said, "I meant what I said about examining everyone who left Giza. I didn't have enough men to go into the desert.

I do promise however, we will find the man who nearly killed you."

"Good hunting, my Lord."

Haka saluted with his fist across his chest.

Alone in the room, Hui sat down. His injury was still sore and made him weak. He sighed and put his feet up on a chair.

Paru opened the door. "I knew you'd still be here. I'll be leaving with the soldiers in the morning. Keep a close eye on my beloved, Hui."

"I promise, my friend. Maybe I can convince her that I am the better man and that she should marry me."

Paru laughed. "Have you been drinking?"

Hui knew Paru didn't suspect his interest in the princess. "I pray the gods go with you. Find the assassin."

The troop ship, *Breath of Shu,* sailed the next morning. She carried fifty soldiers, most of whom were veterans of many desert campaigns. Captain Bek, their commanding officer, and Paru worked well together.

"Rest assured, Bek, that you and your men are in charge of this mission."

Bek nodded. "Excellent, but we'll both need every bit of help in finding this demon."

The soldiers spread out on deck, while others found shade under the sail and slept. Each man carried a pack that included a kaftan with a hood, empty water skins they would fill at Giza, a flint, dagger and sandals with extra thick leather soles.

The two officers sat on deck outside the old mariner's cabin. From their vantage point, they could survey the deck and enjoy the river breezes.

"Have you come up with a plan?" Paru asked.

"There's a trail used by merchants we can follow. If we have any luck, the desert dwellers we encounter may have seen our man."

Paru's eyebrows raised. "Could the assassin have been one of them?"

Bek shook his head. "They would have killed a baby born with such a birthmark. They would consider it cursed by the gods."

Both men brushed their forefingers and thumbs across their foreheads to ward off the evil eye.

One of Bek's men brought them a jar of beer, and Paru posed a question.

"Would the assassin head south toward Thinis in the old Upper Kingdom? No, wait. He wouldn't be able to would he? He'd have to sail there."

"Yes, but not with the General's men watching all boats and ships leaving Giza. I think, if it were me, I'd hide out near

Giza and escape when it was safe. He's surely long gone by now."

"You're probably right."

That night, everyone slept on deck. The moon was so bright Paru could see the lines on his hands. He whispered, "Oh, Khonshu, god of the moon, guide us to this evil son of Seth."

Captain Bek heard him, but only grunted, turned over and fell asleep.

At sun up, they sailed south and by afternoon, reached the Giza causeway.

Bek disembarked with his men who quickly formed by platoon to await orders. Paru walked alongside him as he marched his men past the monuments and into the small Giza market.

On the other side, they found the barracks of the local garrison and their sergeant came out to greet them. "I've gathered the camels General Haka ordered, Captain," he said. "We also have additional supplies you might need stored in a tent behind the barracks."

"Excellent, Sergeant. We'll leave at dusk," Bek said. He turned to Paru. "We'll travel at night because of the sun. I'll assign camels to my men. Take one, and learn to handle it. They can be stubborn beasts and have minds of their own."

"Isn't there a horse I can borrow?" Paru asked. "Not one person I know has ever ridden on a camel."

Bek shook his head again. "There's too much loose sand in this part of the desert. The Asiatics proved them to be the best animal for the desert."

"You know best, Captain."

After a supper of fresh fish, steamed vegetables and plenty of beer, the hunt began in earnest. Five scouts rode on ahead and as the moon reached the height of its heavenly arc, they approached a large outcropping of rock. They would have to go around it.

The trail narrowed as they followed it around and into the dark shadows.

One of their men cried out, "Captain! Over here."

Paru and Bek reined in their camels and kicked their heels into the animal's sides. The beasts lowered their front legs first, and in order to keep their balance, then lowered their hind quarters. The officers jumped down and hurried toward the soldier.

"Down there," he said, pointing to a crevice in the rocks.

Bek and Paru made their way down. Many of their men followed behind. Large boulders cast shadows in the moon-light, making it difficult to see the ground. Paru stopped, stunned.

"By the gods!" Bek exclaimed. Lying at the bottom of the rock formation were the bodies of the five scouts. They were covered in blood, and by the light of the moon it was evident their throats had been slashed. Their life's blood drained onto the thirsty sand. Several vipers slithered away from the bodies and back into the shadows.

Paru and the men quickly made the sign against the evil eye.

In the distance, a jackal howled, and Paru felt a chill course down his spine. Anubis, the jackal-headed god and guardian of the dead, had been there. It was too late for preparations for the afterlife. The five warriors' final journey could never begin.

CHAPTER EIGHT

Captain Bek stood on a mound of sand with Paru at his side. His arms were crossed, and a look of concern showed on his face. The cool night breeze blew across the depression between the large boulders scattered there by some great underground upheaval.

"Bury them," Bek commanded. "They deserve to be laid to rest and not left to the jackals. Hurry."

The deaths reminded Paru of what it meant for a soldier to die far from home. Their lives ended in the sand with only stones to mark their passing.

"Our assassin is not alone, Bek," Paru said. "I hadn't counted on there being a band of them."

Bek said, "We will press on."

The soldiers used their daggers to dig deep graves for their comrades. Then, wrapping the warriors carefully in their kaftans, they raised the hoods on them to protect their heads and laid them respectfully into the ground. Placing stones over the bodies, they then filled the graves with sand. More stones taken from around the rock formation covered the graves.

"That should keep vultures and predators away." Bek said.

Paru addressed the men. "Pharaoh will see that each scout's family receives money to live on for a year. This I promise in his name."

The soldiers showed their approval by striking their swords against their shields.

"Mount up!" Bek ordered. "We're on our own now, so keep your eyes open. Check every shadow that moves. There are so many tracks, we can't count them. There's enough moonlight for your archers to bring down anything they spot."

The noise of so many camels surprised Paru. Horses could be loud, but the camels definitely exceeded them by all their rude and loud sounds.

"It would help if we knew how many were in their band," Paru said.

"I agree. It must be large. They were able to overcome five of our warriors without any sign of a struggle. We must continue to advance. My men want to avenge their comrades."

"I can understand that," Paru shouted.

Bek gave the order to advance, and the column of camels headed west.

Behind them, a faint glow on the horizon announced Ra's imminent arrival.

In the royal palace at Thebes, Pharaoh welcomed Iset back. "There you are, you beautiful creature! You've stayed away too long."

Iset howled in response, making the king laugh.

"She's saying she's sorry, Majesty," Hui said.

"Well, she should be, Lord Chamberlain." Khafre picked her up and carried her into the front room.

The queen walked toward them. "Iset, welcome back. Oh, and it's good to see you too, my Lord Hui. Your chest is healing, I trust."

"Majesty. I'm doing better. Lord Ameni has done wonders for me."

"Well, *Lord Chamberlain,"* Princess Hettie said, entering the front room eating a pear. She caught some of the sweet juice with a small linen cloth.

"Good morning, Princess," Hui replied.

"Any news of the search?" she asked.

Hui shook his head. "Paru and his men have only been gone three days, Hettie. We would have received a messenger pigeon if they'd found anything."

He turned to Khafre. "Majesty, may I speak with you privately?"

"Hui, you know I don't like to discuss affairs of state at home." Iset jumped down as Pharaoh stood. "Is it important?"

"Forgive me, Majesty. It is."

Outside on the veranda, Khafre stood at the railing studying the river below. The palace dominated a high hill overlooking the city. "Tell me why you disturb my pleasant morning?"

Hui waited for Pharaoh to sit before taking his place on a polished granite bench facing his majesty. "It's Thinis, Great One. There are rumors at court that the old families of the ancient southern kingdom are displeased."

Pharaoh frowned and pulled on his goatee. "Thinis again." He sighed and closed his eyes. "My mother was born there, and so was my older brother Djedefre. When she married Khufu, my father, it was another way to show Egypt the north and south were united."

"That explains a lot, Majesty," Hui said. "But it does not explain why they would send an assassin to kill you."

"Revenge, my friend. When my brother died mysteriously, they blamed me."

"I see. I don't wish to cause you pain, Great Egypt, but will you tell me what happened to him?"

Pharaoh stood and paced along the railing. "It was a sad day. Djedefre invited me on a hunt south of the city. There were two other nobles with us who were also avid hunters—Lord Harua and Lord Kames. The captain of the guards organized the hunt and brought along twenty of his men. We sighted several antelope and my brother and I circled around them, he to the right and I the left."

Khafre paused and his expression turned sad. His brow furrowed and his eyes took on a dark look. "I took aim and released my arrow and saw the animal fall. The captain of the guards sent his men to retrieve the antelope, but on the way one of them cried, 'Pharaoh's been hit! Hurry.' When we reached my brother, he was gasping his last. An arrow had pierced his heart."

"I'm so sorry, Majesty," Hui said.

"What I didn't understand Hui, was I knew my arrow struck that antelope and when we pulled the arrow from it, it had my personal markings. No one doubted that someone else fired the shot that killed Djedefre, not me."

Hui ran his hand across his forehead. Pharaoh's words puzzled him. "Forgive me, Majesty, but did you treat members of your brother's court badly after you became Pharaoh? Did you give them any other reasons to hate you? Dismiss any generals or councilors?"

"No, but many of them left on their own."

"Then I don't understand why they would want to take their revenge after so many years."

"Only the gods know why, Hui."

"What about members of your brother's family? Where are they?"

"Djedefre's queen died a month after he did. The physician said it was a stomach ailment, but my wife is convinced she died of poison. Djedefre had no son to succeed him and his only daughter died of a fever when she was little. As the only brother, he knew I would succeed him as did the court."

Hui shook his head. "Something is not right."

"I agree, Nephew. Let us pray that Paru and his men find the answer."

Fighting the desert wind, one of Bek's warriors shouted, "I think I know where these tracks are headed, Captain. They're racing to Fayouin, the great lake. It's the only water source. They should be there by now. From it they can sail out onto the river and disappear south."

Paru shifted in his saddle. "We're wasting time here. We must head for the river and commandeer a ship."

"At the lake we can ask the villagers what they saw," Bek said. "They should be able to give us some clue as to who these men are."

The thin clouds in the eastern sky resembled an unfinished painting of purples, and reds and pinks.

"We must keep going even in the daylight. We have no choice," Bek said.

"Thank the gods for these hoods," Paru grumbled.

Ra, the glory of the sun, pushed through the clouds in a burst of light increasing the morning heat to unbearable levels.

"Sir," one of the soldiers said. "I found this back there when we stopped to relieve ourselves." He held up something to show his commander.

"Move closer, Sati. What is it?" Bek asked.

"It's a Bedouin scarf I think, Captain."

Paru rode over to examine it. "What is that symbol?"

"Where?"

"There, in the center. It looks like the bones of a spine."

"I don't know, Sati. Show it to the rest of the men. Someone might recognize it."

Sati saluted and did as ordered. He returned a short time later. "No one knows, Sir."

"All right—let's go on," Bek said. "We're heading for the Fayouin." He shouted over his shoulder, "Someone in the village along the shore might recognize it."

Their long line of camels advanced and a strong wind sculpted the sand like waves on the sea. Paru pulled his hood closer to keep the sand out of his eyes.

By sunset, the men reached a small village by the lake, the largest in Egypt. It stretched for miles and a small estuary connected it to the great sacred river. The men dismounted on its banks, threw off their clothes, and jumped into the cool fresh water, washing away all the sand.

"Watch out for crocs and hippos!" Bek warned.

When he and Paru approached the village, an elderly man greeted them. He insisted they sit with him by the fire.

"We are looking for some men, father," Paru said.

Using the polite respected word for elder made the man smile. "You are the second band of men to pass through here today," he said. "But yours is the largest."

"What can you tell us about the first group?" Bek asked.

"There were about two dozen men, but they were cloaked so it was hard to see their faces. They stopped to fill their waterskins."

"Did you know who they were, father?" Hui asked.

"Yes, but I wasn't sure at first until I saw one of them wearing the sign."

"The sign? What sign?" Hui asked.

"It was on the headscarf, and I recognize the sign of the Djed. You know—the symbol that looks like a man's spine."

Captain Paru glanced at Bek. "The Djed, as in the name of Pharaoh's brother—Pharaoh Djedefre?"

"Yes, that's it," the villager said. "It is also an honored emblem on banners and flags of the old kingdom of the south. It was long before you men were born."

"Thank you, friend," Bek said. He and Paru returned to their men.

"What should we do?" Paru asked.

"We'll ride to the east of the lake and take a ship to Thinis. There's a small fort here at the lake where we can leave our camels. They'll take them back to Giza."

Paru returned to the man by the fire. "How far to the garrison, Old One?"

"Perhaps five miles," the man replied.

Paru gave him a copper coin and thanked him for the information.

"All right men," Bek shouted. "We're moving ahead to the local barracks. We'll leave our camels with them."

A great shout of jubilation filled the air, and Paru smiled. "I agree with them," he said. "I'm covered with fleas from this beast."

Bek laughed.

Their caravan of soldiers rode toward the southern end of the lake. There, they found the army barracks and the men were glad to leave their camels with the soldiers on duty. Now on foot, they marched by platoon around the south edge of the lake. By mid-day, when the sun stood directly overhead, they found a ship large enough to carry them south to Thinis.

"We would like to commandeer your vessel, Captain," Paru said. "I am Captain of Pharaoh's Guard and need to reach Thinnis as fast as possible. His majesty will pay our expenses."

"I am Khaba, my Lord. It is an honor to serve his majesty. We've finished unloading our cargo so we can sail when you're ready."

Bek marched his men up the gangway and let them settle on deck. Khaba offered his cabin to the two officers, but they refused, preferring to sleep on deck with their men. The condition of the ship revealed its considerable age. The hull's weathered planks of wood, daubed with pitch at the joints had ropes binding them together. Dozens of patches sewn on the large horizontal sail made it resemble an old family quilt hung out to dry.

"I just hope it'll get us there," Paru mumbled.

In the capital, Hui found Pharaoh in the side dressing room connected to the Hall of Audiences. Servants helped him with the double-crown of Egypt and his ceremonial jewelry. "Majesty," Hui said. "We've received a cryptic message from Captain Paru. It arrived by messenger pigeon."

"Merowrrr..." Iset sounded like she was scolding him.

"Iset! What are you doing here?" Hui said. "Has she been following you everywhere, Great Pharaoh?"

"If she wants to, let her be. What is the message, Hui?"

The chamberlain took out the very small papyrus and read,

"Thinis next. Looking for Djed."

"Is that it?"

"Yes, Majesty."

Iset jumped up onto one of the wardrobes. She looked down at Hui, sat down and began to wash her face with her paws.

"What do you think it means?" Khafre asked.

"Well, the first part is easy. They're sailing to Thinis. We don't know why, but it is a good sign I believe."

"And the part about Djed. It's taken from my brother Djedefre's name."

"It gave me pause," Hui said. "I think it refers to the symbol of the backbone of Osiris. It was used by the southern kingdom and identifies with the Lord of the underworld."

"Humph!" Khafre growled.

"I think it means our warriors are on the trail of those who are behind this return to the worship of Osiris. I recommend Majesty, and I know we are not to tell you what to do, but I would hope you not go near anyone connected to this worship until Paru is back."

"Very well."

"Thank you, Sire. Now your people await your wisdom." Hui opened the door and entered the Hall of Audiences and raised his staff. He struck the floor three times. It was the sign for those in the room to prostrate themselves on the floor.

Hui's beautiful feline walked out, looked at the courtiers and caused everyone to gasp. Iset climbed up the steps and sat down on the arm of the throne.

Hui realized it was too late to remove her. He tapped the floor three more times and announced the entrance of Pharaoh.

Khafre entered the Hall and walked toward his throne. When he saw Iset sitting there—looking directly at him and purring—he smiled. He reached out for her and she jumped into his arms. He sat down and the cat moved to her favorite spot on the king's shoulder.

Hui tapped the floor once more and the people stood. The first petitioner was instructed to approach and stand before the king.

Hui overheard two of the priests talking near him. They were there to represent the judgment and wisdom of the gods.

"Do you see that? There is a cat on the throne," one whispered.

The other said, "Pharaoh is favored indeed to be visited by the very presence of the goddess Bastet. She stands for mercy and charity. It is a good sign."

Hui had to suppress his smile lest the courtiers think him irresponsible. He admired Iset sitting on the throne of the most powerful man in the world—as if she was entitled to be there.

When each petitioner approached, she jumped down, walked over and sniffed them. Then, she returned to her place on the arm of the throne. She would then meow and stare at the king.

Pharaoh would then grant the petition.

If Iset yawned, yowled or hissed, at a petitioner, he denied their request.

Hui thought, Iset, Queen of cats and Pharaoh's friend. Who would have thought it possible?

At the end of the morning, General Herihor entered the hall to speak with Pharaoh.

Iset became so agitated she hissed at him. She jumped down and hid behind the throne until the general had gone.

Pharaoh stood and everyone in the hall prostrated themselves again as he left.

Hui walked to the throne and picked Iset up. Together they entered the small dressing room where an attendant was removing the king's double crown and his red cape.

"Did you see how Iset reacted to General Herihor?" Hui asked.

"Yes, I couldn't understand that. What caused her to behave so?"

"Majesty, I swear before all the gods, she only does that when I am in danger. She's trying to warn you but will tell you in her own way and time."

"Now you make me nervous, Chamberlain. Has she ever been wrong?"

"Never, Majesty."

CHAPTER NINE

"By the carbuncles on Seth's backside! If I stay cooped up on this ship one more day, I'll go mad," Bek growled.

The merchant ship sailed up river for three days. The soldiers grew weary of their cramped quarters but food was plentiful. They savored the fresh fish grilled over the crewmen's small stoves. At each stop along the way, they brought fresh bread, dates and clay jars of beer onboard.

Captain Paru should have been tired of the journey, but found it surprisingly pleasant. The music of the old ship itself, with its creaking boards, the scrunching and twisting of ropes holding the planks together, and flapping of the great sail soothed his nerves. He propped his right foot up on the lower railing and enjoyed the shoreline passing by. The occasional small group of children ran to the river's edge to wave and shout a greeting. He waved back and laughed with them. Sporadically, a chorus of angry hippos snorted protests when disturbed. The river meandered, ran past a sheer wall where vultures rested, then flowed away from the cliffs. Soon a long semi-circle of mountains stretched before them.

Reaching Thinis late on the fourth day, the ship's captain anchored far from shore. "I have to wait for a berth before docking."

Early the next morning, with the fore and aft anchors raised, the rudder men guided the ship into port. The smells of stale fish and spoiled vegetables greeted them. No crowds gathered on the empty dock.

With the ship squared away, the crew lowered the gangway. An officer from the local garrison walked up to greet them. "I am Cheres, friends. Welcome to Thinis." He saluted, and they returned the greeting. He led them along the riverbank to the nearby army garrison.

After his visitors took a seat in the small office, Captain Cheres leaned back on the rear legs of his chair. "Your message by carrier pigeon said it was an urgent matter. How can we help?"

Paru leaned forward. "Captain, we are on a mission for Pharaoh. An attempt was made on his life and we are in pursuit of the group who tried to kill him."

Cheres frowned. "May they be cursed. Who would dare such a thing?"

"Sons of whores, that's who," Bek exclaimed. "Five of my best men are dead, and the Lord Chamberlain seriously wounded. A village elder in Fayium told us that the men we're looking for wear headbands bearing the mark of Osiris. They say it is the symbol of an ancient group called the Djed and that they were from here."

Paru sensed the officer's attitude change immediately. His eyes shifted nervously and he wouldn't look directly at his visitors.

"Djed, you say. Yes, we've heard of them. They were a violent group of thugs who were disbanded many years ago."

"Disbanded?" Bek's exclamation reflected his anger. "Then how do you explain this?" He pulled the Djed headband out of the waistband of his kilt and threw it on the desk.

Cheres's chair moved forward. "Seth's breath! I thought I'd never see that again. I can't believe it. Pharaoh's army wiped them out. I swear in his majesty's name."

Bek scowled. "Well then, the god of the underworld has brought them back with a vengeance." He stood and walked over to the only window in the room. A hot breeze from the desert forced him to turn back.

Paru said, "Where can we begin our search for them?"

Cheres took some time to respond. "It will be difficult for you, I'm afraid. The people here were loyal to your Pharaoh's brother—and some still are. While they did not approve of this band of Djed, they supported their cause and their loyalty to Pharaoh Djedefre."

Paru frowned. "You said, '*Your* Pharaoh,' as if he was not *your* Pharaoh, Captain. Need we question your loyalty to his majesty?"

Pursing his lips, Cheres' eyes narrowed and glinted as if filled with fire. "I owe my appointment to a member of Pharaoh Djedefre's family. I cannot do anything against them."

"Your lack of cooperation will not please his majesty," Bek growled.

"Arrest him," Paru insisted.

Bek shook his head. "No, our fight isn't with these men." He paused, and then added, "Captain Cheres, you and your men are confined to the barracks until we return."

Cheres stood. "You can't do that."

Paru stood. "You are outnumbered, I'm afraid. Tell your men you are under orders from his majesty."

Cheres left his office. Paru and Bek could hear the officer's men complaining as he explained what was going to happen. They turned and walked back to their ship.

Bek stood with his hands on his hips. "Follow me, men. We'll camp near the governor's residence. If we're not received by him, we'll return to the ship."

Bek's men groaned, but followed the two officers off the ship. They marched in units toward the town center. On the way, Paru asked a passerby how to find the governor's house. The man pointed to a large white-washed villa on a small hill on the other side of town.

Abruptly, Bek stopped. "Have you noticed? There's no sign of welcome. It's as if the people know why we are here. What's wrong with them?"

Paru wiped sweat from his brow. "We're the old enemy, remember? We come from the Lower Kingdom. My father taught me ever since I could remember that we were one Egypt, united. But what I've seen today denies that."

Upon reaching the villa, their eighty guards and soldiers stood outside the wall while Paru and Bek approached the front gate. Several house guards blocked their way.

Paru approached and raised his hand. "Stand aside. We are on Pharaoh's business."

The largest guard leaned toward him. "You will not pass." The other three drew their curved swords, holding them at the ready.

Bek raised his hand high over his head, signaling to his company. "Ready," he shouted. His men drew their swords and stood prepared to fight. "Shall I give the order?" Bek asked the governor's guard.

"Hold," Paru said. "To avoid a blood bath, escort the captain and myself to the governor."

The guard nodded to his comrades and they put their weapons away. "Follow me," he grumbled.

Bek turned to his sergeant. "Keep the men at the ready."

Bek and Paru walked up the steps to the front door. A tall heavy-set nobleman opened it, frowning at the strangers. "What is the meaning of this intrusion?"

Paru saluted. "We come in Pharaoh's name, my Lord Governor. I am Captain of the Royal Guards, and Captain Bek commands the army troops now standing outside your gate. Why this hostility toward Pharaoh's men?"

Bek stepped forward. "A message was sent to the captain of your garrison. He knew we were coming."

The governor turned away. "I received no word of this, Captain. But enter and follow me." He led them out onto the patio and encouraged them to be seated.

"I am Governor Reseph, Gentlemen." He took his place on a limestone bench opposite them under a lemon tree. He picked up his black and white cat which began to purr as he pet him. "Now tell me what this is all about. I received my appointment as governor from our great Pharaoh himself. I will do all I can to help you."

Paru forced a smile. "Thank you, my Lord." He went on to tell him the whole story. "You can surely understand why we must find these assassins and bring them to justice." As he spoke, Paru noticed that the governor showed no expression whatsoever, only nodding from time to time. When Paru finished, Reseph stood and paced about.

The lines on the governor's face showed a strong determination. "I can't believe the band of Djed are back. I'm from this region, Captain—born in a village only two miles from here. These are my people and their hostility stems from the way Pharaoh Djedefre died. It is an open wound that will not heal." He turned to face them. "Horus help us. What can we do?"

Captain Bek cleared his throat. "We need to know their hiding places, my Lord. Will the people help us? Will you?"

The governor shook his head. "I cannot betray my people. Pharaoh can do with me as he wills, but I cannot." He paused and crossed his arms. "As to where they're hiding, there are so many places for them to vanish. Like desert foxes, they know every burrow and cave out there, especially in the rocky lands to the east. But you won't find them. The people have warned them. They don't trust northerners. That's just the way it is."

No one spoke for some time. Finally, the governor sat down.

Paru looked at Bek who could only shrug his shoulders.

The governor broke the silence. "Here's my advice, officers. I believe someone in Memphis is behind this resurgence of the old band of thugs. Examine those closest to Pharaoh—everyone—lords, ladies, generals, servants—all of them. As the gods are my witness, there is a traitor in your midst."

Paru scratched his chest. "It sounds impossible to us, my Lord, but we will do as you say, *after* we've hunted out any foxes or jackals that have gone to ground."

Bek stood. "Your future, Lord Governor, does not look promising. I cannot leave the deaths of five of my men unavenged. Even now, Pharaoh's chamberlain lies gravely ill from their attempt on Pharaoh's life. No, we will not withdraw until we have done everything to bring the killers to justice."

Paru said, "Order Captain Cheres to stand down, Governor. If he refuses to cooperate, then they are confined to their barracks. They are not to leave or interfere. We outnumber them four to one. Is that clear?"

The governor frowned.

Paru suppressed a smile. He was certain the wealthy nobleman was not accustomed to young men telling him what to do.

The governor raised his hands as if in defeat. "I will do as you say." He then escorted them to the door.

Outside on the street in front of the governor's villa, Bek and Paru's troops stood to attention. This time, word of why they were there must have spread, because as they walked back to the river, the streets were empty

Bek grinned. "Word gets around."

Over the next two weeks, four teams of warriors searched every cave and canyon in the surrounding cliffs. Their hopes

of finding the band of Djed diminished as they returned to the ship each night empty-handed.

One afternoon, as the teams met around an old well on the edge of the desert, a Bedouin child walked into the camp. The boy, perhaps seven summers old, had no fear of the soldiers.

One of Bek's men exclaimed, "Look, what's in his hand?"

The boy held a dagger, pointing it at the men.

Another warrior said, "That's Gebal's dagger."

Captain Bek rushed toward the boy. When he saw the weapon the child was holding, he turned around. "By Seth's shadow, Paru! This belonged to one of my scouts."

A soldier took it out of the boy's hand and gave it to Bek. The boy reached into his small robe and took out a piece of sheepskin. He walked toward the man to whom the soldier had given the dagger and handed it to the officer.

Bek unrolled it so he and Paru could read it. The message, in Egyptian, read:

> ***"Leave Thinis. Only the usurper's Blood can cleanse the curse."***

Bek handed it to Paru. "Can anyone speak Bedouin?"

A young soldier stepped out and stood beside Bek and the boy. "I can, Captain,"

"Ask him who gave him the dagger and scroll," Bek ordered.

The soldier knelt on one knee and asked the question. The boy responded softly.

"He says, Captain, they called themselves sons of the true Pharaoh."

"Now ask him where his village is."

After more mumbling from the boy, the soldier said, "In the tents over there, Captain—near the cliffs that resemble a camel's back."

The lad turned to leave, but soldiers blocked his path.

Bek waved his hand. "Let him go, men. His people won't tell us anything."

The men parted and the boy hurried away.

A strong wind blew in from that direction, stirring up the sand, forcing the soldiers to cover their eyes.

Paru turned his back to the wind. "We should head for the ship. A sandstorm could be coming." When they moved out, Bek walked next to him and he sensed his comrade was troubled. "Take courage, friend. We could probably stay here forever and not learn any more than we already know. I'm even more concerned for the safety of Pharaoh and his family. We should go back. I feel we are needed at home."

Bek nodded. "I'll tell the men to prepare for departure in the morning." They walked a bit farther before Bek added, "I know my men feel as I do. We've failed Pharaoh and it will mean death for us all."

Paru frowned. "I understand, but you forget that my good friend is Pharaoh's Lord Chamberlain. I'll ask him to intercede for us."

In Memphis, Hui grew anxious. There had been no word from Paru in several weeks and Pharaoh asked him constantly for the latest information. Princess Hettie invited him to the palace for the mid-day meal. The three of them sat together in the dining room—the princess, Hui and his cat.

Iset meowed as Hettie placed a tin plate with a small sardine on the floor.

"I can hear her purr across the room," Hui said. "You're spoiling her."

Hettie's servants brought them slices of freshly baked bread and goat cheese.

Hui spread spoons of honey on his bread, and chose fresh dates from a silver plate.

Hettie's beautiful forehead wrinkled. "Where could they be, Hui? I'm, worried."

"They could already be travelling back on the river," Hui said. "Don't worry about your beloved. He can take care of himself."

"I know, but allow me to worry, brother. It pleases me."

His stomach tightened at her use of 'brother.' Hui wanted to be more than that. He changed the subject, asking about her older brother serving in the Army of the North. "Where is Menkaure serving now?"

"He is at Kadesh, at least according to General Herihor," she said. "I miss him, ever since he and father had a falling out a couple of years ago. He left the palace a few months before you became chamberlain."

"I remember, Highness. As Crown Prince, he will succeed your father. I would think Pharaoh would want him here at court to learn everything he can about governing the kingdom."

Hettie frowned. "Oh, be quiet. Menkaure is a soldier. That is all he knows. You are meddling again."

"I didn't mean to. I only met him twice when my father invited him to his villa. He probably doesn't remember me."

"Probably not." She stretched her arms as if thinking. "If only father and he could resolve their differences."

"Merowrill…" Iset interrupted and began to prance in a circle.

Hui's eyes widened. "Something's got her attention."

"What is it?"

A servant rushed in surprising them, making Hui and the princess jump. "Highness, there is a message for the Lord Chamberlain." Hettie nodded, and the man approached, handing Hui a small rolled up papyrus.

"It's come by pigeon," Hui said. Unrolling it, he read it and smiled. "They're headed home, Hettie. Now how did Iset know that?"

The cat meowed again and continued to spin around happily.

Hettie smiled. "Bastet the goddess has made her dance like that."

Hui grinned. "You must be right, Highness. She does that when she's happy."

Clapping her hands, Hettie spun around. "I feel like dancing too. Paru is coming home."

"Yes, well, let's hope he has something good to report to your father."

Paru and Bek arrived at the palace two days later and received an immediate audience with Pharaoh.

Hui met them and escorted them to the Audience Hall. He dismissed all petitioners and courtiers, leaving them alone with Pharaoh.

When the two captains finished their story, Pharaoh scowled and stood.

"Kneel," Hui whispered to them and the two officers knelt on one knee, fists across their chest.

"You have failed me," Khafre growled. "You did not find the assassin. I should send you to the gold mines in Nubia."

The king crossed his arms and Hui recognized the unfavorable reaction.

Paru didn't look up, but said, "We believe, Majesty, the traitor is here in Memphis. If we find him, we'll be able to destroy them all."

Hui decided to risk his own life. "Punish them by making them find the traitor. Use them, Majesty. They have learned more about these jackals than anyone."

Pharaoh sat down on the throne again. "I cannot believe it. A traitor here in the palace, you say?"

Paru, still on one knee said, "Yes, Great One. When we discover who he is, we'll finish the band for good."

Khafre rubbed his shaved head. "Pray Horus helps us find him."

Just then, Iset sauntered into the Hall. Hui could tell she was still acting strangely. She started toward the king, but then approached Hui. She didn't meow as usual. Instead, Hui bent down and lifted her up. "What is it princess?"

Iset made a strange sound and wiggled until he put her down. Circling him, she spat out something at his feet.

"What is it?" Pharaoh asked.

Hui squatted down and looked at the object. Picking it up, he wiped it on his robe.

"It's a ring, Majesty." He stood, approached the king and handed it to him.

"I did not know cats retrieved things."

"Yes Majesty. She loves to find shiny objects and brings them to me. She hides them all over my house."

Pharaoh examined the ring closely and exclaimed, "It is the mark of Djed! Look."

Paru and Bek approached and he passed the ring to them.

"It's the Backbone of Osiris all right," Bek said. "I find it repulsive."

"The question is," Khafre said, "where did Iset find it?"

Hui said, "She has the run of the palace, Majesty. It had to have been here. It will be hard to narrow it down. How could someone be so careless as to lose such an incriminating piece of jewelry?"

Khafre sighed and scratched his small beard. "It is sad to think there are those here who would wish us harm. The queen must not hear any of this."

"Of course, Majesty. Hettie too must not know or she'll tell her mother."

Hui sighed. "There's no way to keep such a secret. With so many looking for the evil band, your court is bound to find out."

Pharaoh nodded. "We will keep what we discover between us four." He motioned for the officers to stand.

"Understood, Majesty," Bek replied.

His majesty stood, walked over and took Iset from Hui's arms. He caressed her and she snuggled her head against Pharaoh's bare chest, patting the golden falcon dangling on his necklace. "Lord Chamberlain, your task is to find your cat's hiding places. Who knows what else she's found!"

At home, Hui's search to find Iset' secret caches wasn't easy. Having grown up in the house, he was certain he knew everyone. He purposely hid shiny coins, a brass thimble loaned him by Kebi his housekeeper. He also gave the cat two old copper rings he no longer wore.

After searching for two days, he found only one item—the thimble. To her, it was all a game. She watched him crawling on the floor looking for holes in the walls or a secret hiding spot under his bed. As he sat on the divan, he was about to give up when the cat jumped onto his lap and dropped something.

"Ah, what have we here, little lady?" He picked up the object and examined it closely. It was a round piece of lapis lazuli. "I've seen this before," he mumbled, and then he remembered. There was a small hole where a piece of string passed through the bead. "The princess has been looking for this for a long time," he told the cat. "During one of her visits, her bracelet broke and I helped her pick up the beads. We found them all but one."

"Bad cat, Iset. You found it and hid it away didn't you?"

"Meowrrr..."

"I know you're sorry. I'll give it back to her.

During the next weeks, Hui, Bek and Paru met privately with palace servants and members of the court. They wanted to learn more from those who had served Pharaoh Djedefre. The best information, in Hui's opinion, came from the high priest of Ra, Lord Maya.

"Djedefre's reign was difficult," the priest told him. "We liked Pharaoh's brother. He was a warrior who spoke plainly and held values we priests admired."

Hui nodded. He and the priest had entered the temple garden to enjoy the peace and quiet. Hui had come with Pharaoh earlier for a service to honor the God of the Sun. When Khafre left, the elderly holy man invited the chamberlain to enjoy some refreshment.

"Why was his reign difficult, my Lord?" Hui asked. "I remember my father—let us remember his name—liked Djedefre and told me he was a good ruler."

Maya said, "We honor your father's name."Then he continued, "He and Khafre didn't get along. The brothers were constantly competing for their father's love and attention. When Pharaoh Khufu died, they tried to outdo each other in honoring the old king's memory. As a warrior, Prince Djedefre spent his whole life serving his father in the army. He spoke and thought in military terms. In many ways, it made him a strong leader."

"And his brother?"

"Khafre served only a short time in the army. He was and still is a scholar. He spent years at the Academy of Awen. That was the problem between them. Khafre always tried to reason out a problem—Djedefre was a man of action. Consequently, they began to distrust each other and Djedefre consulted his younger brother less and less."

"It's getting late, Holy One. Thank you for your insight into these matters. Pharaoh is fortunate to have such faithful advisors."

"And understanding friends such as yourself, Lord Chamberlain."

Hui bowed his head to the priest, and left the temple. A royal charioteer awaited to drive him back to the palace. When they were about to leave, Hui saw Paru rushing toward him and gave the order to stop.

"The worst has happened, Hui!"

"What's wrong?"

"The band of Djed have struck again. They've taken Hettie's brother!"

CHAPTER TEN

Hui leapt into Paru's chariot and held his breath as his friend raced to the palace. They ran up the steps and passed through the larger number of guards now surrounding Pharaoh's residence. Paru followed him, but Hui told him to wait in the hallway until he knew what was happening. Guards outside the golden doors admitted him and he found the royal family distraught.

Hettie ran to him and they embraced. He inhaled her wonderful fragrance and held her close. She sobbed and lay her head on his chest. "Oh, Hui, I went to his room and he was gone. The note on his bed had blood on it."

Pharaoh asked who was at the door, and Hui said, "It's me, Majesty."

"Come into the family room, my boy."

Hui entered, bowing his head politely.

The king nodded to him. "Read this, Nephew."

Hui took the blood-stained papyrus and read:

Remember Djedefre.

Pharaoh's face was flushed with anger. "And now they prey upon innocent children? By Seth's entrails, I will kill them all!"

Queen Persenet wept and Hettie put her arms around her mother but couldn't stop her crying. She helped her up and walked with her to the queen's bed chamber.

Pharaoh walked over and pushed open the door leading to the veranda. He stood with his fists on his hips. Hui recognized the posture as evidence of the king's frustration and followed him out.

Below, the eternal river shimmered in the sunlight. A skein of geese trumpeted in chorus above them as they flew in formation low over the city.

Pharaoh paced back and forth and then stopped at the railing. "How did these nameless sons of filth get inside, Hui? They snatched my son from the most secure place in the kingdom." He struck his fist hard into his other hand. "I want to kill someone with my bare hands!" He turned and faced his chamberlain. "I want Captain Paru arrested! He failed me in every way. Why did his guards not protect my son? He allowed assassins to enter our home and take him while we slept. We might all have been killed."

Hui let the king vent his anger and frustration. He could not defend Paru. "I pray Prince Dua is safe, my Lord King. The blood on the letter may only be from the struggle when Dua tried to defend himself against the kidnappers."

Khafre's face lit up. "What did you say? Kidnappers? Yes, yes, you could be right. Kidnappers always ask for a ransom do they not? There may still be hope."

"Yes, Majesty. We must believe Horus, the sacred Protector of the Pharaohs, will come to his aid."

Hettie returned and joined them. "Mother is lying down. She is exhausted from shock and worry. I have asked the physician to give her a sleeping potion."

Pharaoh nodded. "Thank you, Hettie. Stay with her."

Unfortunately, at that moment, Captain Paru walked out onto the veranda and knelt on one knee, his fist across his chest in salute.

Seeing the expression of anger and contempt on Pharaoh's face, Hui quickly moved and stood next to the officer.

Pharaoh rushed toward Paru. Grabbing the officer's short sword he held it to the young man's neck. "Call the guards,

Hui. Arrest him. I want nothing to do with this traitor." He raised the sword and was about to strike Paru but Hui did the unthinkable and stepped between them.

"Stand away, Hui, I want him cut to pieces before my eyes, I swear before Horus!"

Hui called for the guards, who rushed in. "Arrest the Captain. Take him to Pharaoh's prison for execution."

Hettie was about to protest, but Hui took her hand and led her back inside. He whispered, "Don't say anything. We'll try to save him later. Right now, your father has every right to be angry with him. I'll intervene when he's more reasonable. Go to your mother."

Hettie nodded, her eyes full of tears. She glanced again at Paru, before wiping them away with her sleeve as she left.

Four guards grabbed Paru and escorted him out. He glanced back at Hui and shook his head.

When Hui returned to the king, he found him sitting on the bench next to the railing.

In a quiet voice he said, "Forgive me, Majesty. I should not have tried to stop you, but he is my friend and Hettie's too."

Pharaoh waved his hand, ignoring his comment. "If they kill my son, Hui, Prince Menkhare, my eldest, will succeed me. Since our estrangement, he is a son I no longer know and refuse to make crown prince."

Hui frowned and walked to the edge of the veranda. "The gods cannot be pleased, Majesty. Seth, the god of darkness has upset Maat, the eternal balance. I cannot tell you what to do but I would suggest you order General Haka to secure the palace. Let no one in or out. We will question your staff, Majesty. They may have seen something. I promise we will discover what happened."

A soft mewing called from somewhere in the palace. Pharaoh looked for the source, and walked toward it. "It is Iset, but where is she?"

"Over there, my Lord." Hui walked toward a small metal screen at the bottom of the living room wall. It covered a ventilation shaft that allowed air into the apartments. Hui removed a cord that held it in place and Iset pranced out. She brushed against Hui's legs before walking over to the king.

"Meow..." She sat down and looked up at Pharaoh, bent her head lower and opened her mouth. A small round object fell to the floor.

The king picked it up, and wiped it off. "What is this?"

Hui took it and knew immediately what it was. "It's the top of a dagger, Majesty. The kind our soldiers use. That small round bit is always coming off. It must have fallen off one used by the prince's kidnappers."

"Thank Horus. We need to find the warrior who is missing that piece and we will have our man."

Hui didn't object, but was already thinking about how many soldiers there were.

Pharaoh picked up the cat. "Iset deserves a reward, Hui. Take her to the kitchen and find her a treat."

Dua couldn't see. A cloth band wrapped around his head covered his eyes and mouth. He was bouncing up and down on a camel and found it difficult to breathe. Another strip of cloth covered his mouth. At fifteen summers, he was small for his age. The thugs had tied him onto the beast, and he tried to figure out where he was. He could smell the lush vegetation of the river nearby, but couldn't tell in what direction his captors were taking him.

One of the men grumbled. "He looks like his uncle, doesn't he? Look at his forehead and that nose."

"Who cares?" another replied. "We deliver him and the gold will be ours."

Dua heard someone else shout. "How much farther, Amasis?"

"We'll be there by nightfall. It won't be long now, so keep quiet."

Dua felt groggy. They'd made him drink something which made him dizzy. He'd fought them, but one of the men struck him hard on the back of his head and he passed out. He felt blood trickle down his face, but it had stopped. They had removed his narrow gold crown and wide armbands. They cut off his princely braid with its woven gold ornamentation. The ring with his personal cartouche was taken as well as his golden belt—gifts from his father.

Dua whispered under his breath. "Horus deliver me from these jackals and sons of Seth." Tears threatened, but he fought them back. He was no longer a child, but a Prince of Egypt. Where was Captain Paru and his royal guards? When he returned, he'd make sure that his father punished them.

A voice up ahead cried out, "There it is."

Dua's camel stopped and someone loosened the ropes that held him in the saddle. Rough hands pulled him down and yanked off his blindfold. Blinded by the bright sunlight for an instant, he peered through squinted eyes. Ancient ruins of a temple surrounded their camp. Broken columns lay on the sand and only a small portion of the building remained.

A large man laughed and made a comic bow. "Welcome to your palace, Prince." The speaker was dirty and his clothes torn and rough. "Bring him with you, Ibi. Watch him closely!"

Dua tried to determine by their speech where his abductors were from. They wore strange headbands but their words were not any northern dialect he knew.

As one of them built a fire, another arrived, riding a black horse. He dismounted and joined the others. He was much taller than they. "Where is the prisoner? That foul son of Khafre?"

The man closest to Dua pushed him forward. "Here he is, Sheshanka."

The leader tore the cloth from Dua's mouth.

The prince spat at him. "Father will kill you! All of you!"

The men laughed and the leader struck the young man on the mouth. Dua winced as the pain started to throb.

"Look at his face, Chief," the man who had ridden with Dua said. "Who does he look like?"

The leader studied Dua up close for the first time. "I see, yes. He does look like his uncle Djedefre—we remember his name."

"Djedefre lives," the gang repeated.

When Sheshanka turned to face his men, Dua sucked in his breath. There, on the back of the man's shaven head was the blue birthmark. This was the man everyone was looking for.

"Thank you Horus," he whispered silently.

In the quiet of Hui's house, a loud knock awakened him from a deep sleep. It was dark outside and he stumbled groggily to the door, opened it and found Paru's sergeant.

"He's gone, Sir! He's run away!"

"Who? What? Excuse me sergeant, I'm not yet awake."

"Captain Paru, Sir. He's broken out of prison."

Hui had to sit down. "When?"

"In the middle of the night. My men must have helped him break out."

"Come in, Sergeant."

"Meorwl...hiss...hiss...spittttt."

"It's all right, Iset. He's a friend."

"Mmmmrrr?"

"Yes, now leave him alone. Come out to the kitchen, Sergeant Nafi. My housekeeper doesn't come until morning, so I can't offer you anything but beer and bread."

"Beer please, my Lord."

Hui sat at the table with the soldier, drank some beer and yawned. "Why didn't *you* help him escape, Nafi? You're his sergeant."

"I think he did not want me to know so that I could take charge of our men when he left."

"I see. Where do you think he is headed?"

Nafi took a small piece of day-old bread from the basket on the table. "One of my men reported that the Captain had a lead as to where the kidnappers may have gone."

"Great news. Do you know where?"

Nafi shook his head. "Mmmm—mmmm," he mumbled, his mouth full of bread. "Some old ruin."

"Gods, man! Egypt is covered with ruins!"

"What can we do, Sir?

"If I were you, Sergeant, I'd take some of my men and get out of Memphis as fast as I could. Leave before Pharaoh hears the news. Try to bring him back."

"I'm going now, Sir, but I thought you should know."

"Thank you. Pray the gods help you and Paru find the prince."

Nafi saluted and hurried out.

Paru and his friends didn't stop riding until they'd put five leagues between them and Memphis. They reined in by the riverside so their horses could drink and rest. They couldn't build a fire for obvious reasons, but sat around on large rocks.

Paru dismounted and sat on an old broken-off log. "I can't believe you men broke me out. You realize you've made yourselves criminals. Pharaoh will send his troops after us, so the only hope we have is to rescue the prince before they catch us."

His men grunted in approval.

Paru continued. "We can still follow their horses' tracks. It looks like they're heading for that old Temple of Sahure by the river south of here." As he studied his men's faces, he was pleased to recognize his best archers and swordsmen. On this kind of rescue operation, however, he knew the bow would be their best weapon.

A short, well-built guard patted his horse. "Do you think they've already killed the prince?"

Paru shook his head. "They won't harm him until some kind of ransom is paid. There's always a ransom."

Another led his horse to the edge of the river. "We'll have to leave our horses somewhere."

Paru studied the man's troubled face. "What is it Saho?"

"I don't think we should continue on land. Let's use the river instead, Captain. We can canoe to their camp. They'll never hear us coming. Our arrows can pick them off."

Paru nodded. "I agree. Let's camp here for the night, and we can find canoes in the morning. Two will be enough. We'll convince a villager to keep the horses for us." He walked to his horse and led it to water, keeping his eye out for crocodiles. "I like the plan. The kidnappers won't expect us to follow them on the river."

Saho tested the tension of his bow. "How far are we from the ruins?"

Leading his horse to a grassy area near the road, Paru said, "About two miles. When I was young, my family liked to come fishing near here."

Someone grumbled. "When can we eat?"

Paru chuckled. "Ptei, you're always hungry. At sunup, one of you can buy bread and dates at the village market. I'm sorry I didn't have any money in prison."

His men laughed. They stretched out on the grass and looked up at the stars.

Paru crossed his arms behind his head and whispered, "Hettie, my love, I pray the gods your brother's still alive."

The youngest among them sighed. "I hope we seven can take them."

Paru said so all could hear, "If Horus is with us, we will."

In the morning, just before sunrise, Paru and Ptei left camp. Ptei, to buy food, and Paru went looking for villagers who would loan him their canoes. Receiving two, he rowed back to camp. After they had eaten fresh bread and dates, they loaded their weapons and paddled out into the main current. Paru's canoe was in the lead.

Because of the river's speed, Paru kept his canoe close to shore. No one would spot them hidden in the papyrus and other vegetation. When they reached the ruin, they tied up their canoes. Creeping closer to the old temple, they hid behind fallen sections of the stone columns.

Paru whispered, "We'll split up. Three of you will come from the far side. We'll go from here. Wait for my signal."

Prince Dua had given up hope of anyone coming to look for him. In fact, there had been very little movement of any kind. He remained tied up, guarded by two of the band. Both men held their daggers at the ready.

Sheshanka, their leader, stood brushing his horse and talking to two of his men a short distance away.

Without warning, Dua heard the swish of an arrow fly past and strike one of his guards. Other arrows struck the thugs talking with the leader.

Sheshanka shouted, "Kill the prince," then he leapt onto his horse and raced off.

A guard next to Dua grabbed the dagger from his belt and lunged at the prince, but an arrow struck him in the chest knocking him down.

The prince cried out as the falling man's dagger sliced him in the side. Blood poured out and he tried to stop it with his hands. "Horus, help me."

Paru reached him first and shouted, "Strips of cloth! Hurry!" His men rushed over, tore their clothes and began to wrap up the prince's wound.

"Keep pressure on it," Paru ordered. "Carry him to the canoe."

Four men lifted Dua and ran with him to the river. Paru jumped in beside Dua and one of his men, while the others took the second.

As Paru turned and put his paddle into the water, an arrow struck him in the chest with such force, it knocked him over.

The young guard turned and yelled, "The Captain's hit."

The other canoe came along side and two men helped lift Paru into their canoe. Dua heard the still conscious officer shout in gasps of breath, "Row out of here. I can breathe and I'm not bleeding. Get the prince away. Head for the village."

The last thing Dua saw before passing out, was the arrow sticking out of Paru's chest.

CHAPTER ELEVEN

Though in shock, Captain Paru still heard and saw everything. The men of the rescue team kept pressure on the prince's wound, and tried to prevent Paru from moving. When they docked, other guardsmen ran and brought stretchers to carry the wounded up to the palace.

Someone shouted, "Call the Physician! The Prince is wounded." Their cries echoed through the halls.

Lord Mitry, the physician, rushed to the injured men, ordering them taken to his surgery inside the royal residence. Paru's eyes widened as the healer cleaned and sewed up the wound in the prince's side. He gave the young lad plenty of wine to dull his senses. His horsehair stitches were far enough apart to allow the swelling that would occur after such an injury. Fortunately, Paru remained conscious and watched it all as if detached, feeling no pain.

Pharaoh rushed in and stood beside his son. His eyes showed concern and fear. He addressed Paru in the other bed. "We are grateful, Captain."

Paru coughed and had difficulty speaking. "I swore Great One I'd bring him home. I only regret he is injured."

The physician moved next to Paru. "Captain, the shaft is too close to your heart and I fear what might happen if I cut out the arrow."

Pharaoh's voice became insistent. "Help him, Mitry. He saved our son."

"Yes, Majesty. I will do my best with incantations and Horus' help."

Paru's eyes followed the physician as he spoke to Hui who just arrived. Paru raised his hand and motioned for him to approach.

Hui leaned over.

Paru struggled to speak. "Call Hettie. The physician is not able to help me. I want to see her before my Ka leaves me, Hui. Hurry."

Nodding, Hui straightened himself and rushed out of the room. He returned with the princess who had been waiting in the hall.

The physician told those in the surgery that he was about to operate. Pharaoh, Hettie and Hui seated themselves out of the way.

Mitry placed his hand on Paru's shoulder. "Captain, the reason you feel little pain is the arrowhead struck your spine, dulling your sensations. If I remove it, your heart will stop and your Ka will leave you to join the gods. I'm truly sorry."

Paru coughed again and his voice became raspy and weak. "I understand. I saved the prince, and that is what I set out to accomplish. This will be a good death for a soldier. I give my life for my Lord and King."

Pharaoh heard and approached the officer's bed. He took Paru's hand and gripped it tightly. "Your sacrifice will be remembered Captain. We will inscribe your name on a panel in my tomb. Your memory and name will live on."

Paru squeezed the living god of Egypt's hand and slowly nodded his head.

The physician said, "Majesty, your servants can carry the prince to his bed. The bleeding has stopped. I'll be up shortly. I've given him pain medicine, but I'll bring something to help him sleep."

Pharaoh nodded and called for the guards to carry his son out of the surgery.

Hettie pulled up a chair and sat beside her beloved. Tears ran down her cheeks as she caressed his face. "Love of my life. Why are the gods taking you from me? I want to be with *you*."

Paru's eyes misted over. "My love for you will never die dearest one. Our Kas will be together." He kissed the palms of her hands. She leaned over and kissed him on the lips.

When she lifted her head, Paru saw Hui standing behind her. "Hettie, I'm leaving you with my friend Hui. He would never tell you, but he's loved you all his life. Be kind to him." His voice weakened and he had trouble forming his words. "Bury me in my village. . . in a tomb that will. . .make my family proud."

Hettie nodded. "Father will honor you, Beloved. Kiss me now so it will last forever."Their lips met again, gently at first, and then with the passion they both felt.

As Hettie sat up, Paru began to cough and couldn't stop. Hettie ran for the door. "Healer! Please help him."

Mitry rushed in and nodded for Hui to lead the princess a few steps away. He gave Paru a small wooden rod. Bite down hard, my son."

Paru did so to keep from screaming as the physician cut the arrow from his chest.

Hui held his hand and squeezed it reassuringly.

Paru tried to focus his eyes on his friend, but then a thick-like fog clouded his vision. Suddenly the spark of life ebbed from him and he felt his friend's hand go limp.

Mitry pressed a cloth down on the wound as the captain's heart beat a few moments longer.

The room grew dark and Paru couldn't keep his eyes open. A golden light pierced the black—he gasped in surprise, and then died.

Hui was saddened that Hettie didn't speak to anyone during the seventy days of Paru's embalming. She took her food in her room and mourned the loss of her love alone. Her brother's wound had healed nicely and he was proud to show his scar to everyone—especially admiring young ladies.

When Paru's sarcophagus arrived, Prince Dua and his sister followed it down to the royal ship that would carry it to the captain's village. Long narrow blue banners that flew from the ship's mast commemorated the captain's regimental colors. Hui, as Lord Chamberlain, followed on board, as did many of Paru's regiment. Others would have liked to go, but they remained on the dock, singing songs of a soldier's victory.

After the ship sailed, Hettie and her brother came out of the royal cabin and stood beside the solid red alabaster sarcophagus. A slight breeze made the lotus flowers placed on it wave and fill the air with their sweet scent.

Hettie ran her hand along the coffin. "It's beautiful, isn't it Hui? Look how they've carved images of the battles he fought in, and how his name is used for the borders around the lid."

Hui felt the hieroglyphics cut deep into it. His eyes grew large when he felt the letters of Hettie's throne name. He turned to her. "Putting your name here is risky, isn't it, Highness?"

"What? It simply says, 'Princess Rekhetre mourns the loss of the royal family's protector.'"

Hui nodded. "Yes, I see, Highness. It is a beautiful tribute and will last longer than flowers, or an offering of incense." He stopped talking when he saw the tears running down her cheeks. He wanted so badly to wipe them away gently with his fingers.

When they reached Paru's village, a great crowd met them at the landing. People from neighboring villages had journeyed to honor the captain's memory. A new tomb, built by Pharaoh's architects, made the villagers proud of the honor the king had shown for their hometown son.

A great feast held to honor the captain included musicians and dancers who gyrated to the beat of goat-skin covered drums. When the hour grew late, many of the visiting villagers settled down for the night around their campfires. Paru's family stayed behind near the Princess' ship to share stories of their son's bravery and victories.

Early the next morning, Pharaoh's galley departed as the villagers cheered the princess and threw flowers to her.

On the return voyage, the princess avoided Hui and spent all of her time with her brother.

Upon arriving in Memphis, the king summoned his daughter to his council chamber. When she entered, she found only her father and mother present.

Khafre spoke formally. "Enter, Daughter. Your mother and I wanted to meet you in this official way because it is a concern of the court. We have learned on our own, that you and Captain Paru—of pleasant memory—were in love. Is this true?"

Hettie didn't respond and her mother said, "Tell him, Daughter. He means you no harm."

"Yes, Father, it is true." She gasped and controlled a sob. "Part of my Ka has gone with him."

Pharaoh frowned. "We would never have allowed such a marriage."

"I know."

"Your mother and I insist you seek our approval from now on."

Hettie's eyes filled with tears. "I don't know, Father, Mother. I have always respected your decisions. However, the last two men associated with my name are dead and so is my heart. I will not be seeking to marry any time soon."

Pharaoh stood and approached her. "Come, child. Walk with me."

Servants and courtiers bowed and smiled as they passed, but Hettie's heart stiffened because of her father's insistence on what she believed was simply a charade.

Later, in her room, she found Iset sitting on her bed, licking her paws.

"Meoww?..."

Hettie sat next to her and Iset stopped washing, looked the princess in the face and nudged her head into Hettie's side.

"Thank you, Little One." Hettie hugged her companion for a long time. She had told Hui she needed Iset for emotional support, and he agreed.

"What mischief did you get into while I was gone, little one?"

"Meorrrrlll...?" The cat jumped off the bed and disappeared into another room.

Hettie removed the robe she'd worn to meet her parents, and put on a soft gown for the night. She lay on the bed staring at the ceiling paintings of the river with its flying ducks and stars.

"Mewwwuuu..." The cat leapt onto the bed and placed an object close to Hettie's wooden headrest, which the princess preferred to the soft pillows many Egyptians were adopting.

"What is it little sister?" She picked up a small piece of papyrus still rolled up. The cat must have found the scrap near a scribe's desk. There were always small pieces of discarded papyrus lying on the floor. When unrolled she discovered two words: "...his death."

The cat must have found the scrap near a scribe's desk. There were always small pieces of discarded papyrus lying on the floor.

The next day, when she showed the scrap to Hui, he dismissed it. "It could have been part of a letter about Paru's death. We don't know. I am surprised that Iset has widened her interests from coins and rings."

Hettie remembered her beloved's words about Hui and they made her uncomfortable now around him. She'd never felt like this before. She liked his companionship, but her feelings about him confused her.

Hui spoke quietly. "Your father needs a new captain of the guard. I don't know who to recommend. Who can replace Paru? I miss him more than I thought I would."

His words surprised her, and moved her so much, she couldn't speak. She simply nodded.

He thought a moment and said, "Yes, well, I think what you need, is to get away from this place. Somewhere that will help you take your mind off things—a journey perhaps. Why not an excursion on the river?"

They were still in the family living room, and Hettie walked out onto the veranda. A light blue morning fog had not yet dissipated blurring the view of the city. "A journey. . ." she repeated.

Hui followed her out.

Hettie's face lit up, and color returned to her cheeks. "Hui, it is a wonderful idea. A trip down river would be wonderful.

I've never been to the Middle Sea or Great Sea as the Asiatics in the north call it. I wonder if father would approve. My brother could come with me, although Father might not be willing to risk his life again with the assassin still at large."

"I could go with you, if you'd like. I've not been that far north. My father once said you cannot imagine the size of the sea. You could also visit the Academy at Awen—the center of all knowledge. I don't know, however, if Pharaoh could spare me from court for two weeks. Such a journey would take at least that long."

"To get away from all the bad memories would be a good thing, Hui. Will you put in a good word to father?"

"Of course," he said, bowing overdramatically. "I'll speak to him about it tomorrow."

Iset rubbed against his shins until he picked her up.

"Hello, beautiful lady. I've missed you. You've been in the palace a long time."

"Meow..." Iset purred contentedly and closed her eyes

Hettie said, "I think she's missed you. It was kind of you to let her stay."

"I've missed her, but you needed her more. I'm glad this clever, independent cat has adopted you too."

Hettie laughed. "She's still hiding things you know." She turned to face him. "Oh, I just remembered. I have something to show you." She went to her bedchamber and returned with the small piece of papyrus.

"How odd," Hui said. "Hmm. '***his death.***' Interesting." He scratched his head. "It could be something. Do you mind if I show this to the chief scribe? He may recognize the handwriting."

"If you want to. I thought Iset only collected shiny baubles and coins."

"So did I. Another mystery—just like her."

The cat made a growling sound, causing Hui to chuckle. "I think she feels insulted."

The elderly scribe examined the piece of papyrus. "I don't know, Chamberlain. So many letters are dictated by the king every day."The Chief Scribe looked at it closely front and back and shook his head. "Leave it, and I'll remember."

"Thank you Lord Raad. It may be nothing, but we need to be extra cautious these days."

"Agreed."

One of the guards approached. "My Lord, His Majesty commands your presence in the Council Chamber."

Hui nodded, thanked the scribe again, and followed the guard down the long hallway connecting the many rooms of the palace.

When he entered, he bowed his head. "Majesty."

"Hui, there you are. Sit down."

"What is it, Great Egypt?"

"I'm having trouble selecting a new officer to lead the Guards."

"I see. Who are the candidates?"

"Well, there's Sergeant Nafi of course. He's a good man," Pharaoh said. "But there is also Captain Ansra from General Herihor's staff. He speaks very highly of the young man and he does come from Thinis. I thought this might please our brothers south of Memphis."

Hui nodded. "Yes, I can see that. It is perhaps a wise move at this time, Majesty."

"You said 'perhaps.' What does that mean?"

"Apologies, Great King. I was only thinking how courageous Nafi was in saving your son. He knows all the protocol of the court. I'm sure Ansra is capable too. You don't need my opinion, my Lord. You are Pharaoh. You cannot make mistakes."

"Ha! Try telling that to the queen."

Hui's laughter began as a reluctant chuckle and then rose in volume to fill the chamber. The king joined him.

Khafre said, "You've made a good point about Nafi, however. I'd still want him here in the palace. Dua would like that."

"Nafi's a warrior first, Sire and will follow orders. You make the decision. The gods will guide you."

"I respect your advice. That is why you are chamberlain. Just now, when you laughed, you sounded like your father—we remember his name."

"His name honors me, as do you Majesty. You do so beyond reason."

Pharaoh stood, pleased with Hui's words. He nodded to him and left the council chamber.

When the sun reached its highest point, the king sent the steward to invite Hui to the king's table at mid-day. Only he and the princess joined Khafre for a light meal of eggs, goat cheese, bread, wine and fruit.

Hettie spread fresh honey on the warm bread and Hui followed her example. He much preferred dipping the bread into the honey jar, but remembered at whose table he was sitting.

Pharaoh took a peach, cut it and removed the pit. "You know, Even I have never been to the Great Sea—I, ruler of the world. We are told by our wisest men that there are sea monsters beyond our sacred river."

Hui smiled, and looked at the princess.

Khafre asked, "Why would you suggest such a journey for my daughter, Hui?"

"I did not mean to offend, Majesty. I simply thought it would do her good to get away from the capital for a while."

"I agree, believe it or not."

Hettie raised her eyebrows. "Oh, do you, Father?"

The king smiled, but then his face took on a mischievous look. "Now who will go with you?"

Hettie looked first at Hui, then her father. "You know, Father. I already told you."

"I know. But can Egypt continue without its chamberlain? The court can continue without me—but not its chamberlain."

The two young people grinned at him.

Pharaoh raised his hand a little. "No, no, it is not amusing. I'm serious, Hui. What will I do during the weeks you are away?"

Hui was ready with an answer. "Lord Tathra, the Keeper of the Royal Seal, already knows what I do as chamberlain. For the present, there are no disputes between Nomes, nor are we at war with anyone. It might be a good time to permit Prince Dua to sit with you and learn how to be Pharaoh. I'm not as indispensable as you might think, Majesty."

Khafre sighed. "I will reluctantly allow it, but I warn you, the position of chamberlain might be filled when you come back."

Hui looked at the king's face and relaxed. The king was grinning.

"The queen will insist Hettie's attendants travel with her, as well as a large number of guards for her protection."

"Of course, Majesty."

"I will send Captain Ansra with you. I have made him Captain of the Guard and you'll tell me how he does."

"As you command, Great House."

Pharaoh stood, and left the dining room.

Hettie stood and her expression changed to one of displeasure. "Oh, you men can be so vexing at times. I don't need a babysitter, Hui. Why must so many guards come with me?"

Hui stopped her. "Be kind to your father, Hettie. He's lost one son because of some disagreement, and almost another through a kidnapping. Can you blame him from being concerned? Accept his conditions. You'll have a good time and we can take Iset along if you want."

"Then I'll go," she said. "Let's leave in two days."

"Agreed. I'll make the arrangements."

As Hui left the royal apartment, he walked to his office near the Audience Hall. He found the Royal Scribe waiting for him.

"I knew I'd recognize this handwriting, Lord Chamberlain. It's General Herihor's."

CHAPTER TWELVE

On the great ship, Iset fussed and mewed. She wanted out.

Hui knew the cat didn't like the fiber basket he'd put her in. "It's the best way for her to travel," he explained to the princess.

Hettie frowned. "Let her run around, Hui. She's a free spirit." She still felt the loss of Paru. During the long period of mourning and then his burial, she had grieved alone, not wanting people around her. Hui finally helped her out of her sad world with the idea of the voyage. She still felt edgy and her patience left her easily.

"We can't let her run free," Hui said. "When the ship's underway, she might fall overboard and become crocodile dessert."

"Well then you can let her out when we're docked or anchored for the night, surely."

"Yes, of course. I'm sure she would be safe in the cabin."

An officer interrupted. "Forgive me, Highness. The ship is preparing to sail. Do we have your permission to get underway?"

Hettie ignored him. "Lord Chamberlain, who is this person?"

"This is Captain Ansra, Highness, the new officer in charge of your Royal Guard."

Hettie turned to face the stranger. "You should know *Captain* that I've been sailing on my father's ship since I was five summers old. I know more about how to travel on board this ship than you will ever know. I would say your new command has not begun very well."

Ansra bowed his head politely. "Forgive a foolish guardsman, Highness. I should have known better."

"Carry on." She turned away from him, waving her hand in dismissal.

When he had gone, Hui said, "Give him a chance, Hettie. We know you want to be alone, but it takes a while for us mere mortals to become accustomed to you goddesses."

She frowned at first but then forced a smile. "Leave us, lowly mortal, or I'll put a spell on you."

Hui mumbled under his breath, "You already have."

"What did you say?"

"Nothing important Highness. If it pleases you, I'll put Iset in your cabin. She can move about and be safe."

She nodded and he carried the cat's basket to the royal cabin and left her inside. He then made his way to the bow as the crew began pulling in the anchors and the gangway. One hundred crewmen readied the great sail and the oars. There was an air of excitement as the great ship readied herself to leave port. Twenty-foot narrow blue banners flew from the mast, flapping in the wind, sounding like a great bird preparing to fly.

A large crowd on the landing waved to the princess. They clapped and shouted her name. Some began to dance as the ship left the harbor.

"Unfurl sail," the ship's captain shouted. The great rectangular canvas fell slowly from the top spar and was lashed in place on the deck.

The captain walked to the helm where his large muscular crewmen stood by each of the three steering oars. Their arms tensed awaiting the captain's command. As the wind filled the sail, the *Breath of Horus* moved toward the center of the river. "Hard to port," the captain ordered. Guided by her rudders, she moved as gracefully as the sacred Ibis.

"Good morning, Lord Chamberlain," the ship's officer said. Permit me to say you resemble in some ways my old friend, your father—his name is remembered."

"I honor his name," Hui recited. "Thank you, Captain Tiakken. I remember you well."

"Permit a question, my Lord. What is wrong with this new captain of the Guard? He's already had an altercation with my crew chief."

"I do not know him, my friend. We've only just met. I must report to Pharaoh whether or not he measures up to his new position."

"You must remind him who is master of this ship, my Lord."

"I'll speak to him. May Horus and the god of the wind grant us a smooth sail."

Tiakken nodded.

The river grew wider as the ship sailed into the main current that carried it north to the delta. Captain Tiakken followed Hui astern and they laughed at the angry bellowing from the hippos as the ship cut through their herd.

Tiakken said, "By tomorrow afternoon we should reach Awen."

Hui smiled. "I marvel at your ruddermen. Look at them. They turn those huge oars as if they were reeds. Their arms are gigantic."

"They have to be, my Lord. Three other men will relieve them at regular intervals. You can't fight the current for long."

"How long have you served his Majesty, Captain?"

"I have sailed in his majesty's ships for fifteen summers." He paused as if searching for his words. "The crew was pleased you brought a cat on board. You must know a ship draws rats and we will be happy to see fewer of them on this voyage."

"Iset is a good hunter, Captain. I should also say the princess wishes to stop at Bubastis. She will pay tribute to the cat goddess."

"The princess is in command of this ship, my Lord. We will do as she wishes."

"Well said. It is up to me to tell Captain Ansra."

Tiakken laughed. "Good luck, my Lord. I think you'll need it."

Hui walked to his cabin astern on the high deck. He removed his nemes headdress, and changed from his long white robe of office to a shorter tunic. He went outside and walked to the royal cabin, knocking timidly at the cedar door.

A lady-in-waiting opened it. "Yes?"

"May I enter?" Hui asked.

"Let him in, Benemba."

Hui entered and as fast as a striped flash of light, his cat flew out the door.

"No!" Hettie cried. Her attendants ran after Iset, but Hui knew she would be impossible to catch.

Hettie rushed out. "I'm sorry, Hui. She was too quick for me."

"Not to worry, Highness. She's smart and has probably already found a mouse-dinner below."

Hettie smiled. “I hope you’re right.” She breathed in some of the cool air blowing from the north. “It’s pleasant here under the awning. Let’s sit awhile.”

“As you wish, Highness.”

After taking seats on cushioned divans, they enjoyed the lush green vegetation passing by. The delta possessed the blackest soil of Egypt and the region boasted rich fields of corn, barley and leeks. Large clusters of papyrus and bulrushes hid colorful ducks and graceful Ibis.

The two ladies-in-waiting interrupted them. Benemba fell to the deck, tears filling her eyes. “She’s gone, Highness. We deserve your whip.”

Hettie looked at Hui and frowned. Speaking in a stern voice, she said, “I will decide what to do with both of you later.” She waved her hand, sending the two women back to the cabin.

Hui grinned. “You are an evil mistress, Highness. A whipping? The poor creatures.”

At that moment, approaching footsteps drew their attention. It was Captain Ansra.

“Highness,” he called. “I must speak with you about stopping at Bubastis. That will not be possible.”

Hettie stood and walked toward him. “We are not pleased, Captain. First, you do not approach this royal deck unless invited. Secondly, this is my ship, not yours. Your actions and words offend us. Leave before we choose to report our displeasure to the chamberlain.”

The captain's face turned red. He looked toward the chamberlain and scowled. With his fist to his chest, he turned and hurried down the steps.

Hui smiled. "Tsk. Tsk. Such royal indignation. Pharaoh would be proud."

Hettie smiled. "Quiet, mortal!"

The deep voice of Captain Tiakken called from the bottom of the steps. "This lady belongs up there, Chamberlain."

Hui jumped up and rushed to the steps. "Iset. Bad cat."

The Captain handed her to him and she jumped up onto Hui's shoulder. Upon regaining his seat beside Hettie, Hui said, "It was a mistake to bring her. I'm sorry."

Hettie leaned closer and Iset jumped gently onto the princess's lap. "Ah, see. She wants to make up." She ran her hand along Iset's smooth short hair and the cat purred contentedly.

"Tell me what you think of the new captain of the Guard?" she said.

Hui took a moment to reflect. "To be fair, it's too soon for an opinion. He started off on the wrong foot with you and the ship's captain."

"I agree. Please keep him away from me."

"As you command, Daughter of Pharaoh." He got down on one knee like the guards and slapped his chest with his fist. She laughed and the sweet sound of it touched his heart.

The royal cousins spent the rest of the afternoon talking about their childhood and games they played around the palace. As Ra approached the western horizon, the princess retired to her cabin for supper. She fed Iset minnows caught by the crew—a reward for her rat catching.

Hui ate a few pieces of fruit in his cabin, and then went outside to stand at the railing. The palette of the sky above included deep reds and magenta. Finally, the black night erased the canvas.

The princess walked outside and joined him.

A slight breeze passed over them. Hui inhaled the fragrance of Hettie's bath oils and seductive jasmine perfume. Being near her every day was going to be difficult.

"I love this time of day," she said.

"I do as well, Highness. It's as if Ra's chariot has left behind clouds in all the colors of the rainbow."

"Uh hum. I'm glad we've anchored far enough away from shore. No insects to trouble our sleep tonight."

It was not insects that would trouble Hui's sleep. He turned ever so slightly toward her. "Goodnight, Cousin. Pleasant dreams."

She nodded and was about to leave. "You know, my father used to tell me that if you see a cat in your dreams, it is a good omen and what you wish for will come true." She smiled at him before walking to her cabin.

When the door closed, he whispered, "Happy dreams my love."

Awen, the great city of learning, stood where the sacred river split into seven streams. Each one flowed through the great delta and carried precious silt and nourishment to Egypt's largest garden. Visitors from many lands beyond Egypt came to admire the mighty temple of Ra. The City of the Sun also gave birth to the Royal Academy where students were taught not only academic subjects, but astronomy and discoveries in medicine.

Hui had sent a message ahead by pigeon to announce Hettie's arrival. A large crowd welcomed the ship and awaited the princess' appearance.

Captain Ansra approached the royal deck and insisted he speak with the princess.

Hui said, "I hope you've learned how to speak to her."

"Let me do my job, my Lord. Her safety is *my* concern."

"If she doesn't trust you, Captain, how can you keep her safe?"

The officer pursed his lips and didn't reply. He walked to the cabin and asked to speak with the princess. The attendant closed the door and a few moments later, the princess opened it and stepped out.

"Yes, Captain?"

Ansra saluted. "Highness, the high priest of the temple is coming to accompany you. The guards will go with you to carry your chair. We anticipate no trouble with the crowd and hope your visit will be a pleasant one."

"Thank you Captain."

Ansra saluted, turned and walked back down to the main deck.

Hui joined her. "Was he contrite enough, my Lady?"

"Not yet."

When the crowd on shore recognized Pharaoh's daughter, they cheered. She stood at the railing and waved to them. A dozen priests brought a golden carrying chair to the landing. They stopped at the gangway and lowered it.

Hui and the princess walked down the steps to the main deck and stood where the blue carpet covered the ramp.

The high priest walked up it slowly and fell prostrate before the daughter of Pharaoh.

"Thank you for coming, my Lord Priest," Hettie said. She motioned for him to stand.

Hui marveled that the man could even move. He must have experienced eighty summers or maybe more. He was so thin Hui was certain if the wind was too strong, he would blow away. His pleasant deep voice made people around him relax.

It also pleased Hui that the crowd knew Hettie's name. They shouted it as she stepped into the ornate gold carrying chair.

"Rek-het ray, Rek-het ray," they cried, and it soon became a chant as her guards lifted her, and her party moved away from the ship.

Iset rode with the princess. One of the crewmen had made a small leather collar for the cat. Several of the princess' thin golden necklaces linked together made a satisfactory leash.

At the magnificent Temple of the Sun, Hui stood beside Hettie's chair as the guards lowered her to the ground. He whispered so only she could hear, "His name is Ra-Seneb, my Lady."

She nodded. "Thank you."

The high priest and his guests entered the sacred shrine and two young women brought gifts for the princess to present to the god. Ra was at the top of Egypt's pantheon of gods, and the divine name incorporated into the names of the pharaohs. Her father's name, Khafre, meant '*appearing like Ra*.' A huge statue of Horus-Ra stood on a pedestal in the center of the large sanctuary. The eyes of the great falcon appeared to penetrate to the Ka of each person who approached bearing offerings.

Hettie presented gifts of gold and incense, and after Lord Ra-Seneb invoked the blessings of the god on Pharaoh and his family, he led them into a beautiful oasis-like garden. After Hui and Hettie took their places, the priest addressed the princess.

"You have brought a beautiful servant of Bastet to the temple, my Lady. The goddess would be pleased."

Hettie petted Iset on the head.

"Meowlllrrr…"

"This is Iset, Lord Ra-Seneb. She belongs to the Lord Chamberlain, but my family has adopted her too."

"She's beautiful," the priest said. "Will you be visiting the city of cats on your way? Well, that's what we call Bubastis now. It is quite an unusual place."

Hui nodded. "It is our intention, my Lord. We want to pay homage to the goddess for bringing Iset into our lives."

"I understand. Would you like to see our tower of the sun, Highness? You might find it interesting, although I know women may not be able to understand such things."

Hui winced as a spark of fire ignited in Hettie's eyes. Her voice had an edge to it. "Of course, my Lord. We weak women must struggle out of our bondage of ignorance. It may surprise you that this woman can read and write."

Lord Ra-Seneb fell on his face before her. "Forgive me, Royal One. I misspoke. I did not mean to offend."

"Stand, my Lord. Your comment angers me because it reveals old prejudices against female intelligence. I will not pass along your remark to her majesty the queen."

The old man blubbered on the ground until Hui helped him up. "Show us the tower, my Lord. We are both anxious to see it."

Captain Ansra who had been standing at the entrance to the garden shouted, "No. The tower has not been inspected, my Lord Chamberlain."

"Thank you, Captain. Your concern is noted," Hui said.

Hettie grew more offended with the Captain. "Don't you realize you've insulted the High Priest? To assume a faithful priest loyal to my father would seek to harm us is offensive. Lead on, Lord Ra-Seneb."

Anger filled Ansra's eyes instead of regret for what he had done.

Hui said, "Bring only six of your men, Captain."

Ansra grumbled, "Very well."

Seen from everywhere in Awen, the tower was the tallest building. It was as high as an obelisk and made of polished white limestone.

As they began the climb, Hettie passed Iset to Hui and the cat jumped onto his shoulder.

The priest said, "The heavens are best seen at night, of course, Highness. Up here, the stars are brighter than when we look from the ground through mists and dust." He led them up the steps and Hettie was soon out of breath. Lord Ra-Seneb, however, was doing better than everyone.

"Ah," Hui said. "I have to rest." He said so because Hettie needed time to catch her breath.

The priest said, "We're half-way, my friends. It is a difficult climb, especially if you're not accustomed to it."

After a few minutes rest, they continued and it wasn't long before they reached the top of the observatory. Lord Ra-Seneb walked over to a lever on the wall and pulled it.

A round copper ceiling split in two, and the two halves slid down into the stone wall.

Iset dug her claws into Hui's shoulder, frightened by the noise overhead.

"Oh," the princess said. "We are so high." A large stone step enabled her to look out over the city. "It's amazing, Hui! You must look. This is what it must be like from the top of a pyramid."

"I can see the moon rising," Hui said. "Over there above the river. It's shrouded in the river brume as if covered by a veil."

"Imagine how bright everything would be at night," the priest said.

Iset jumped down and sniffed around.

As Hui stepped from the stone, he saw something lying on the floor. He picked up a piece of papyrus and handed it to the priest. "One of your students must have dropped this."

The priest opened the folded papyrus and said, "No, this is addressed to her Highness."

"Let me see," Hui said. He felt the blood drain from his face as he read the message written on it:

"The Princess will die"

At the bottom of the papyrus was a drawing of the symbol of the backbone of Osiris.

"Gods," Hui exclaimed. "The Band of Djed again."

CHAPTER THIRTEEN

"Let me see it," the princess ordered. She grabbed the note and read it. "What does it mean, Hui?"

"It means those who killed Paru want to harm you, Highness. We must turn back."

Hettie turned to Lord Ra-Seneb. "We will go back to our ship. Awen is not as welcoming as we thought."

"Forgive us, Highness," the priest said. "We didn't know."

Captain Ansra said, "Come, my Lady. Your guards will take you out of here." He started down the steps, and she followed with Hui behind.

"Meow..." Iset whined.

Hettie stopped, turned around and handed the cat to him.

He pet Iset to calm her but he could feel her little heart racing. "There, there, little lady. You'll be all right."

At the foot of the tower, Captain Ansra's men awaited to carry the princess back to the ship. The return to the *Horus* would be fast and without ceremony. Instead of thanking the high priest, Hui took him aside and used his most authoritative voice. "I'm afraid, my Lord, that such an affront to Pharaoh Khafre will cause his wrath to fall on every official in Awen."

The priest fell to the ground extending his arms toward the princess. "Please, my Lady. Tell him we plead for mercy. That threatening message was not our doing. I was as surprised as you were. I did not place it there, nor did any of my staff, I assure you. You have to convince him, I beg you."

Hui motioned for the priest to stand. He walked back and forth as if considering the man's predicament. "I know that, my Lord. It came from assassins known as the Band of Djed who oppose the royal family. They nearly killed Pharaoh when he passed below the feet of the Great Lion at Giza. Instead, the arrow struck me and could have killed me. So I know what these men can do."

Lord Ra-Seneb made the sign against the evil eye, crossing his forehead with the forefinger and little finger of his right hand. "May Ra and Horus protect you, my Lord."

Captain Ansra's men surrounded the chair, and lifted it. Hui had given Iset to Hettie who sat nestled in the princess' arms. As they moved away from the tower, no crowd followed them. Afraid perhaps of being associated with those who would harm their princess.

After walking back on board, Hui told Captain Tiakken to set sail for home. "The princess is in danger." The captain nodded, and gave the order to sail south.

Hui headed for the royal cabin, but his head filled with conflicting thoughts. His first inclination was to return to Memphis as quickly as they could, but first he wanted Hettie's thoughts. He knocked on the cabin door.

The princess opened it holding Iset. "Enter." She waved her attendants out.

"But Highness. . ." Benemba protested.

"Leave us," Hettie ordered.

The two women frowned at Hui and left.

"I've told the captain to head for home, Hettie," he said. "It is the only safe place."

"No," she said. "Turn us around. If this Band of whoever wanted to kill me, they could have done so. This is only a warning and I choose to ignore it."

Hui walked to the window and shook his head. "Please Hettie. As your friend, I assure you that you are in danger. Your father was almost killed, then Paru. Please don't let them take you, too."

She sat down and let Iset climb onto her lap. She moved her hand slowly over the cat's soft short hair. Iset closed her eyes in contentment.

Hui turned back to face her. "You know even if you make it a royal command I'll still ignore it. Your father has trusted me with your life. I cannot violate his trust."

"I know, and I understand,"

Iset looked up at the princess's face and touched the royal chin with her paw. "Merrrow…?"

"I want to reach the Great Sea, Hui, and the city of sacred cats. It is our royal wish that you turn the ship back north. It is not a command, because then you would be guilty of disobeying." She paused and then said, "I'm asking as a friend."

"I will not promise, my Lady, but I will talk with the guards and make my decision. It is I who must answer to Pharaoh." He walked over to her and scratched Iset behind the ears before leaving the cabin.

Ansra met him when he reached the main deck. "What you've done is right, my Lord. We must go back. The Princess's safety must come above everything else."

"What did you understand about the threat she received, Captain?"

"Why, only that someone wants to harm her, my Lord. What do you mean?"

"Who sent her the message?"

"We don't know. There was no signature, Lord Chamberlain."

"Not true, Captain. It's signed by the Band of Djed using the Backbone of Osiris as their signature."

Ansra appeared confused. "Who are they? I've never heard of them."

Hui said, "I've seen the name before at Giza and Thinis in the south. They swear to end the reign of our Pharaoh. The backbone they use is the symbol of Osiris, the patron god of the old Southern Kingdom."

Ansra frowned. "Why have we not heard of these assassins before, my Lord? No one has ever mentioned them. I don't understand it."

Captain Tiakken approached and overheard their discussion. "I've heard of it gentlemen. The symbol of the Djed, or pillar of Djed, is used by some as an amulet for the living and the dead. It is placed near the spines of a mummy which is supposed to ensure the resurrection of the dead, allowing the deceased to live eternally."

"Why don't I know this, Captain?" Hui asked.

"My grandparents were born in the Southern Kingdom, my Lord. I say this respectfully—you would have to understand their traditions."

"I see," Hui said.

"Is the princess all right?" Tiakken asked.

Hui said she would be fine, and then added, “I’m sorry for this, Captain, but we are asking you to turn the ship once more and head for Bubastis as she wants.”

“What?” Ansra interrupted. “But there might be danger ahead.”

“We don’t know that, Captain. The princess has chosen not to be intimated.”

“As Captain of the Royal Guards, I must protest my Lord. This is a mistake.”

“Your objections are noted, Captain Ansra.” Hui turned to the ship’s captain. “Captain Tiakken, her highness orders you to change direction and set sail for Bubastis.”

Tiakken said, “Very well, but it will take some time for us to turn the ship. In the delta, the current is very strong.”

“Good,” Hui said. “I’ll come and we’ll talk later.”

Hui walked with Ansra back to the stairs leading up to the royal cabin. “I told the princess I would only agree to this change on the condition that your guards guarantee her protection. Double up each position—when she is in her carrying chair, and here on the ship. Understood?”

Ansra stood at attention and saluted. “Agreed.”

Hui sensed Ansra’s heart wasn’t in it.

No one told the crew of the *Horus* why they were turning the ship north again. “They think the princess couldn’t make up her mind," Tiakken told Hui. His pale blue eyes were set keenly in a wrinkled brown face and Hui instinctively trusted the man.

"Unfortunately, it was I who couldn't decide what to do, my friend. But she is eager to reach the sea as am I."

"I won't try to understand," Tiakken said.

The older man walked toward the bow and Hui followed. "I like it here on the fore deck. I can feel the wind on my face." He stood above where the ship cut through the river and leaned over to allow the water from the waves to splash on his face. Turning back to Hui, he shook his head like a dog ridding itself of the water on its coat. He cleared his throat. "I would only take the princess to the great temple of Bastet, and perhaps the monument to the goddess in the center of town."

"Very well. The next time you are in Memphis, I'll prepare a feast for you."

The captain laughed. "I'll be there to collect on that promise, you can be sure."

When Hui arrived at the royal cabin, Hettie was having trouble with the cat. Iset didn't like wearing the leather collar, but Hettie was eventually able to fasten it on.

Hettie scratched behind Iset's ears. "There will be too many cats where we're going, Iset. I don't want to lose you."

Meorrrr!" Iset turned away.

"Do you want me to carry her, Hettie?"

"No, she's fine, but we're definitely going to need the leash. I think she's used to it now. I'll take a few treats along."

"Very well. We're almost there. I'll check to make sure your guards are ready."

She nodded as he left the cabin.

Captain Ansra stepped on deck with his men who were readying their weapons and reviewing procedures for the next docking. He glanced up when the chamberlain approached.

Hui didn't trust the officer, but didn't know why. "Are your men ready, Captain?"

Ansra scowled. "We are always ready."

Hui noted the lack of the polite 'my Lord.' He said, "Good, I pray it is so. If possible, I'd like more of your men around the princess's carrying chair this time. People will want to try to touch it and there is no way to predict what a crowd will do."

"I agree, but as I said, we are ready."

Hui thought the officer appeared distracted, not his real self. "Is there a problem, Captain? You don't seem as confident or as sure of yourself as when you came on board."

Ansra remained stone-faced for a moment. "It's just this group of assassins you told me about. Several of my men have heard about them and I don't like what they told me. If they are a subversive band of disgruntled southerners loyal to the old Pharaoh, they could prove a greater threat than anticipated."

"You're right. They refused to accept our Pharaoh as successor to his brother, and that was over ten summers ago."

Ansra frowned. "You must admit Pharaoh Djedfre, Khafre's older brother, did die under unusual circumstances."

The captain's remark surprised Hui. It triggered something in his brain, perhaps a warning. "Even so, Captain, our loyalty is to our Lord Pharaoh. May Horus bless his reign."

Ansra's face remained expressionless as if cut from stone.

Hui made note of his lack of enthusiasm.

Later, as the *Breath of Horus* approached the landing at the city of Bubastis, women on the dock ran into the city shouting excitedly. They knew that the long narrow blue and yellow banners floating high above the mast signaled the arrival of a royal visitor. Within a short time, there were large numbers of women on the landing to greet Pharaoh's daughter. The city, also known as the House of Bast, honored the cat goddess. Many of the women in the crowd carried masks of a cat or lioness held in front of their faces.

"Come, Iset," the princess said. She left her two attendants in the cabin and walked down the steps to stand beside Hui on the main deck. Her golden carrying chair awaited on shore, and the guards filed off the ship to control the crowd.

The loud beating of drums accompanied an orchestra as another carrying chair approached borne by women. The drummers increased the rhythm as a young woman stepped out of the chair and walked toward the royal galley. Her beauty stunned Hui. She wore makeup that accentuated her eyes and with her hair swept back, she gave the impression of a lioness. She stood on the end of the azure-blue carpet waiting for the royal visitor.

Hettie whispered, "I'm not often met by a priestess. I'm a little jealous. Look how young and beautiful she is."

"I should say her beauty fades when compared to yours, Princess, but it would not be true."

Hettie growled. "I will not forget that remark, Cousin. Come, let's meet her." With Iset in her arms, she walked down the walkway to the crowd's roar of approval.

The priestess prostrated herself as soon as Hettie's foot touched the carpeted ground.

The princess raised her hand allowing the woman to stand.

"Welcome, Princess, Daughter of our Great Pharaoh. I, Bektamun, announce that our goddess is pleased by this unexpected honor." She smiled when she saw the cat in Hettie's arms. "And I see the honor is double because you have brought the living symbol of our goddess with you."

"Thank you, Priestess," Hettie said. "This is Iset, my companion, but she belongs to Lord Hui our Chamberlain. It is he who arranged for Pharaoh's ship to pay tribute to your goddess."

"We are grateful, Chamberlain. Even men are tolerated here."

That made Hui grin at her as he bowed his head politely.

The priestess asked, "May I hold Iset, my Lady?"

"That's for her to decide, Holy One," Hettie replied.

The priestess advanced but Captain Ansra and his aide moved quickly to stand next to the princess. Their action caused the priestess to take a step back.

Hettie handed Iset to her along with the golden leash.

"Meow?" Iset mewed. She looked up at the face of the young woman and began to purr.

"There, you see," Bektamun said. "She agrees. Come along, Iset, ride with me. We will go directly to your temple, Lord Chamberlain, Highness."

Hui nodded. His carrying chair awaited him, brought up from the hold with Hettie's. He stepped into it as the musicians and drummers continued. The priestess' chair moved forward. In the distance, a large pyramid-shaped building dominated the horizon.

Eight of Captain Ansra's men carried the princess's chair, with the rest of his fifty guards marching alongside. The crowd threw flowers and cheered her as she passed. White-washed buildings along the promenade added reflected sunlight along the way.

Hui had troubling thoughts of Iset injuring the priestess. But he had no reason to worry. When the three chairs arrived and their bearers lowered them to the ground, the priestess stepped out unharmed. She held Iset up to the crowd of women worshippers who cheered and clapped their hands. They chanted a song praising the goddess. The priestess bore no scratches on her face or arms, and Iset remained still as she handed the cat back to the princess.

"I will officiate, Highness," she said. "An offering has been placed near the image of Bastet for you. The chamberlain sent us a message by pigeon before you left Awen."

"Did he?" Hettie looked at Hui and smiled.

He was pleased she now understood that he had decided to come here regardless of the threat back in Awen.

"You will stand with the men, my Lord," the priestess instructed. "Women are more pleasing to the goddess because of their nature."

Hui's expression didn't change. "I understand, Holy One."

"Princess Rekhetre, welcome to our Great Temple."

Hettie nodded and followed the procession of priestesses that met her.

Inside, Hui marveled at one of the most beautiful temples he had ever seen. Fine paintings of the goddess in many of her feline forms—from cat to lioness—decorated the walls and ceiling. In the center of the shrine, stood a large image of the goddess twenty feet tall. Made by the finest sculptors, it had a smooth finish and every detail was cut to perfection.

As the princess walked forward to present her gift at the altar, Hui studied the assembly of worshippers carefully. Ansra's men stood at attention. The captain himself and his aide walked on each side of her as she moved forward to lay a golden box of jewels at the feet of the giant cat.

The high priestess chanted and waved incense above the offering. Its fragrant cloud rose up and over the crowd filling the temple with its sweet fragrance.

The princess was about to return to her place, when a cry arose from the crowd.

"Bektamun!" several women shouted. They rushed forward and caught the priestess as she slumped forward.

Ansra's men surrounded the princess while his aide rushed to the fallen priestess.

Hui joined them. "What is it?"

Ansra said, "Blood. There's blood everywhere my Lord."

His aide said, "Look, Captain. There's a dagger in her side close to her heart."

Hui said, "Quick, Captain. Send your men to the doors. Don't let anyone leave. Hurry!"

Ansra's men surrounded the princess. She could not have moved if she wanted to.

"By the gods!" Hui swore. "Not again." He looked down at Baktamun's body and cringed as a river of blood flowed slowly up to the base of the great image.

The princess reached out and grabbed him. "Gods, Hui... how?"

CHAPTER FOURTEEN

The royal guards tried to calm the crowd inside the temple with little success.

"Get me out of here," Hettie gasped.

"No, Highness," Captain Ansra objected. "That is what the killers want. By targeting the priestess, they hope to draw you out so they can attack."

Hui agreed. "He's right, Highness. As much as I would like you to be away from here, we must wait."

She nodded and a priestess brought her a chair from one of the rooms off the sanctuary.

"All entrances were blocked right after it happened, Sir," Ansra's aide reported.

"Good. Examine each person closely before letting them go. It will take a long time, but it must be done."

The sergeant saluted and gave the order to his men at the six doors.

One of the women sobbed, "Oh, our blessed Bektamun is taken from us. We have lost our Mother."

A physician, led inside by one of the priestesses, knelt beside the body, but there was nothing he could do.

Four of Ansra's men offered to help move the priestess, but the women became indignant that a man might touch the holy departed. Hui was not surprised when the women carried the high priestess into a ritual cleansing room. There they bathed the body before wrapping it in several linen sheets. Lifting Bektamun on their shoulders, they left the temple and began the long walk to the House of the Dead.

The search among the crowd continued at some length, until a guardsman shouted, "We've got him, Captain."

Hui followed Ansra to a side entrance where two guards were struggling to keep the man on the ground.

"His tongue's been cut out, Captain."

Ansra swore, "Seth's backside! We won't learn anything from him."

Hui said, "He was well chosen for his task don't you think—for that very reason. He can't reveal who sent him." He looked at the man. "Stand him up," he ordered. "Now hold on to him tightly." Hui walked around the man examining him closely. He ordered the man stripped to his loincloth but even then, no mark was there to identify him.

He was about to turn away when he stopped and said, "Wait a moment." He reached out and pulled off the wide brass band to reveal the man's bicep. "There it is—look—the mark of Djed."

"I can't believe it," Ansra said.

"Dress him and bring him to the princess. She will decide his fate."

"As you command," Ansra said.

Hui walked back to where Hettie waited patiently. Women from the temple had brought her a cup of juice and honey cakes. When she saw Hui approaching, she stood.

"They've captured the assassin, Highness. They're bringing him to you. Someone removed his tongue long ago, but he bears the mark of Djed on his arm."

Hettie collapsed onto the chair again with a sigh. "Thank Horus it's over."

"No, Highness, not until they're all caught. You must decide what to do with him."

"No. I refuse to look at him. Remove him to the ship. I will pronounce sentence there."

"Yes, my Lady." He walked back and told Ansra her decision. "Bring her chair and bearers. Place more men around her on the way back. She'll decide on the *Horus* what to do next."

Ansra saluted and gave the orders to his men.

Hettie appeared lost standing there holding Iset in an empty temple at the foot of the great image of Bastet. Hui felt sorry for her. The iron smell of blood mixed with everyone's sweat and the dust made it difficult to breathe. The cat climbed up onto Hettie's shoulder and looked up at the large statue.

"Meoooow?..." she wailed.

Dozens of cats roamed freely in the temple, and they ran toward Iset's voice. Hettie held her in her arms and Iset cried again. Inexplicably, all the cats in the temple stopped mewling. They sat still, facing the princess and her cat.

Hui approached her and Iset jumped to his arms. "Come, Princess, let's get away from this madness." He led her toward the temple entrance.

On the ship, Ansra and the chamberlain stood in front of the princess. She was sitting on one of the divans her attendants placed outside on the royal deck.

"We will not turn back as you suggested, Captain Ansra—not before I see the Great Sea. We are uninjured for a second time. We think this Band of Djed, whoever they are, are simply trying to send us a message. What it is, we have no idea."

Hui waited a moment before responding. "First, Highness, you must decide what to do with the prisoner. Shall we throw him into the river?"

"We've already decided, Lord Chamberlain," she replied, returning to majestic plural because of Ansra's presence. "We have learned while you were searching the crowd, that the cat goddess of this temple often takes the form of a lioness. The women who served with Bektamun told us that several lionesses live in an enclosure near the temple. Feed the assassin to them."

Hui's jaw dropped. He shuddered a little, but then responded. "As you have decreed, Princess, it will be done. Captain Ansra, carry out the order."

Hettie stood. "See that he is alive when you throw him to them, Captain. I want the cats to have the pleasure of a hunt and a good meal."

Ansra responded. "Yes, Highness." He knelt on one knee and placed his fist on his chest. "Please consider turning back, my Lady." Receiving no response, he stood and then walked down the steps to the main deck.

Hettie turned. "You will go as our witness, Hui, to see that our order has been carried out."

"Very well, my Lady. I'll go at once."

Captain Ansra and four of his men led the prisoner back to Bastet's temple.

A group of Bektamun's priestesses met Hui at the entrance. The eldest, her hair streaked with gray said, "Follow me, my Lord Chamberlain."

As Ansra's men pushed the assassin ahead of them, the women cursed him with language that made Hui blush.

A large open enclosure built with limestone blocks stood on the north side of the temple. Several series of steps led to the top of the oval structure.

"Give him to us, Captain," the eldest woman ordered.

Ansra looked to Hui who nodded in agreement.

The guardsmen released the man to them who pushed him up the steps. They cut the bonds around his hands and pushed him off the wall into the enclosure. The inarticulate screams of the man as he hit the ground made Hui clench his teeth.

"You are to witness, Lord Chamberlain," the senior priestess called to him.

Hui nodded and climbed the narrow steps. At the top, he was horrified as several lionesses tore the man apart amid the victim's horrific screams. Hui wanted to cover his ears, but steeled himself to remain still. Mercifully, one of the lionesses bit into the assassin's throat, crushing his larynx, ending his screams. Hui closed his eyes but the crunching of bones and tearing of flesh continued.

On the way back to the ship, he threw up, and had difficulty walking up the gangway. He forced himself back up the steps to the royal deck. He found the princess sitting where he left her.

She motioned for him to seat himself and he let out a long breath. "When your father hears about these events, he won't throw *me* to any lions. Instead, he'll have me cut into little pieces and thrown to the crocodiles."

Hettie sighed. "Wasn't it you who wanted me to go on this journey to take my mind off Paru's death?"

Hui nodded.

"Well, I've not had much time for the past. There's too much happening around me. I've not thought of him once." She paused. "I will admit when I saw the handsome new Captain from a distance, I did have a moment of pleasant memory."

"Handsome? You find him handsome?"

"Oh, do not worry. We admire a statue for its beauty do we not?"

"And you've already placed him on a pedestal, if I know you." He grinned at her and she smiled at his attempt to make her laugh.

It took the *Horus* another day and a half to reach the river's end. As it sailed out into the Great Sea, the brown waters of Egypt's sacred river pushed into the deep blue expanse. The princess and everyone on board marveled at what stretched out before them.

"It is frightening, isn't it?" Hettie said. She and her attendants stood at the railing with the chamberlain. "Look how far the water goes—all the way to the horizon and beyond."

"Oh, I felt something. What was that?" Hettie's lady-in-waiting cried. "Something is making the ship move. Can you feel it?"

Captain Tiakken came up the steps laughing. "It's only the waves, ladies. When the wind blows on so much water, it moves in the direction it is pushed. That's all."

"Oh," Hettie said. "Can it blow the ship over?"

Tiakken shook his head. "Don't be afraid. The ship weighs too much for it to roll over, but I admit, in a storm we are tossed about."

"This is alarming. Any more dangers we should know about Captain?" Hettie asked.

"Well, the rocking of the ship has been known to make some sick, Highness. In that case, it is best to lie down and not eat or drink."

Hettie sighed again. "It is beautiful out here. So much blue sky overhead and the blue beneath. This must be what the birds see. Blue all around you."

Hui heard her as he came up the steps. "Now who has become a poet, Highness."

She laughed and then jumped in fear. "Oh! What is that? There is another."

Captain Tiakken chuckled. "They're flying fish, my Lady. Nothing to fear. They stretch out their fins and sail with the wind. Oh, and they're quite tasty when roasted."

"Over there, Highness," Hui pointed. "Another ship."

"It is different," she said. "It has two sails."

Tiakken nodded. "She's Phoenician, Highness. One of the fastest ships on the sea. Your father needs to build ships like that."

Hui said, "So they're built just for the sea? Not for waters like our beloved river?"

"No, my Lord, they *can* sail to Egypt as well. But they are primarily built for these deep waters."

Hettie left Hui and the ship's captain and returned to her cabin.

A short time later, a shout from on top of the mast surprised them. "Sail ho! And it's coming fast, Captain."

Tiakken hurried down and ran aft. Hui followed.

"By the gods! It's pirates," the captain exclaimed.

"It looks the same as the one we saw earlier," Hui said.

"It's Phoenician all right, but they have rigged extra sails on the two masts for speed."

"Surely they wouldn't attack one of Pharaoh's ships."

"Oh, yes they would," Tiakken said.

Captain Ansra ran aft to see what was happening.

Hui told him. "Get your archers ready, Captain. Let's hope they are as good as they say they are."

"The sun is going down,"Tiakken said. "I don't think they would risk attacking at night." He shouted to his crew, "To the oars, men!"

There was still a good wind and the pull of the oars would help move the great ship south again toward Egypt.

Tiakken pursed his lips. "There's a new moon so there won't be enough light. I'll have to anchor here."

"Are the anchor lines long enough?" Hui asked.

"Yes, I knew we were sailing to the sea, my Lord. We've added to their length."

Hui nodded. "Will they try to close in on us in the darkness?"

"No, they know there are archers on board a royal galley. They wouldn't be so foolish. You better reassure the princess, my Lord. Tell her she has nothing to worry about."

Hui left the helm and headed up the steps. He told the princess their situation and tried to calm her and her frightened attendants.

"They're too far away, Highness, and they won't try anything in the night. Your archers will defend us tomorrow. They are the best warriors in the world."

"You're only trying to make us feel better, Hui," Hettie said.

"Yes, I am, but by your face it doesn't look like I've succeeded."

"A little. Can we trust Ansra to defend us?"

"We have no choice. But I take courage in the fact that our men have been trained by the best officers in Egypt. They and Horus will take care of us."

"Will you take Iset with you?" Hettie asked. "What's wrong with her? She's restless and runs around the cabin as if something is chasing her."

"Of course." He walked over and picked up his cat.

"Here's her collar and leash," Benembra, the lady-in-waiting said.

"Try to rest, Ladies," Hui told them. "Let the ship rock you to sleep."

Leaving the royal cabin, Hui found Ansra and his sergeant drilling their men. Archers took positions along the railing on both sides, while others prepared food on their iron braziers.

"They're drinking beer, Captain." Hui said. "I thought you'd want them to have clear heads."

"It's only a few jars among the men, my Lord. It's to help build up their courage."

"Very well, carry on."

Iset tried to wiggle free. "Hold on, cat. We're almost to our cabin." By then it was dark outside. Only a few lights flickered from the upper deck.

"This is going to be a long night, Iset," he said. When he closed his cabin door, he put her down and she began to run around the room, onto the bed, then the table, the chair and back onto the bed.

“What is wrong with you?” Hui asked. He sat on the bed and waited for her to calm down. She jumped up on the window sill but found it closed.

“Meow,” she cried. “Mrrrr…yowel…”

“Gods, Iset, what is it? You have never acted this way.”

She jumped up on the bed and curled up at his side. She tried to hide her head by pushing against him.

Hui rubbed her head, then her back, running his fingers along her hair. They remained like that until Hui dozed off.

A bump on the hull of the ship jarred him awake. He sat up, went over and opened the window, but outside there was nothing. Thinking it might just be one of the crew he closed the window and lay down again. Iset’s purring lulled him back to sleep.

The small dingy cut through the calm water with ease. Two men rowed slowly and silently, while the other four readied their weapons. The sliver of the new moon had risen, and the large Egyptian ship appeared as a ghostly shadow on the water.

“Easy,” their leader whispered. “We’re almost there.”

They rowed on in silence. “You know what to do. Kill anyone awake as silently as possible.”

The dingy advanced closer and came aft of the ship near the rudders.

From up above them, a rope fell and the men quickly climbed up it. A strong hand reached down and helped them over the railing.

"She's in there," the man said. "Slit the throats of her attendants, but don't harm her. Gag her and hurry back with her."

The man who helped them up led them to the royal cabin and the intruders pushed opened the door. A small oil lamp burned on the table and it enabled them to see and silence the sleeping attendants. They wouldn't have felt a thing.

They shook the princess awake, covered her mouth with a linen cloth then tied it behind her head. She struggled as the men tied her hands behind her and bound her feet as well. She continued to resist, until one of the intruders struck her on the head, knocking her out.

"Hurry, to the stern."

The man's colleagues carried the princess down the steps and along the deck toward the rudders. They lowered her carefully to the man who remained in the dingy. He then climbed up the rope and over the railing. He looked back at the ship whose crew lay sound asleep. He could even hear the sailor high on the mast snoring.

Abruptly, a door opened and someone came out on the royal deck. "Where is everyone?" a man shouted. He ran down the steps to the lower deck looking for anyone.

Hui's mind filled with panic. He raced into the princess's cabin with Iset at his heels, and found the bodies of the two attendants with their throats cut. "No, no, no!" he shouted. The princess was gone—taken by intruders. Iset jumped onto the princess' bed and howled. Gods! What could he do? He rushed onto the main deck and realized why everyone was still asleep. "Drugged," he said.

A noise astern caught his attention and he ran toward it.

A man stood there in silhouette, outlined by the faint rays of the new moon.

"You!" Hui shouted.

Captain Ansra struck him with his fist knocking him down. He raised a small club and hit Hui on the head.

Before he lost consciousness, Hui saw Ansra jump over the railing and into the water. The pain to his head became unbearable and his vision faded. He had seen something important and tried to remember what it was.

Iset ran to him and licked the wound at the back of his head. Between licks, she mewled almost a whine and then purred to comfort hm.

Things began to spin and turn black, but Hui remembered seeing, hidden away under Ansra's arm, the mark of Djed.

CHAPTER FIFTEEN

"My Lord, wake up." a voice called to him.

Hui opened his eyes and groaned. "Ow! My head." He recognized Tiakken. "What happened?"

"Let me help you up, Lord Chamberlain. You've fallen here next to the rudders. You've been knocked out."

Hui rubbed the injury on the back of his head. "Wait. I remember. By the gods! The pirates were on our ship. The princess?"

"She's gone, my Lord. They've taken her."

Hui buried his face in his hands. He couldn't breathe for a moment. "Horus help her. We must go after them. Ready the crew." He had trouble standing and had to hold onto the railing to steady himself.

"They're gone, my Lord, and I have no idea in which direction."

A wave of dizziness overcame Hui. "I must sit down."

Tiakken helped him up the steps to his cabin. "We found Iset wandering around on deck. She's waiting for you on your bed."

When the cat saw him, she jumped down and ran around and around, mewling repeatedly. Then she rubbed against his shins.

"Iset, little Lady," Hui said. Sitting on the bed, he touched his sore head again and saw blood on his fingers.

Tiakken said, "I'll send for Binra. He trained with a physician some years ago." He walked to the door and yelled for one of the crewmen to send the man in.

"First, you must see this, my Lord." He helped Hui walk to the royal cabin. Hui's stomach churned when he saw the princess' attendants lying in pools of blood.

"The sons of Seth wanted to make sure they didn't cry out."Tiakken said.

Binra rapped on the door and entered. He carried a basin of water and carefully washed the gash on the top of the chamberlain's head. "If I were a physician, my Lord, I could sew up the wound. I'll tie a bandage tightly around your head. That's all I can do."

Hui nodded. "I am grateful."

When the young man finished, he left the cabin.

Captain Tiakken walked to the window and studied his crew at work. "We are all dead, aren't we, my Lord? We've allowed Pharaoh's daughter to be taken, and only the gods know what they've done with her."

Hui touched the wound on his head again. "You're right of course about Pharaoh's wrath falling on us. We are doomed. I'm going to ask you to do something important, Captain. Bring me the most senior guard from Ansra's men. The one with the most years of service."

"Very well. I'll send Amkhu, he knows the men well."

"Good."

The captain left and Hui stretched out on his bed. Iset curled up with him and purred.

"Meowrlll..."The cat cried, sounding like a lament.

"I know, Iset, I miss her too. Pray to your goddess to save her."

Hettie opened her eyes, and for an instant, didn't know where she was. With her hands tied behind her back and her legs bound, she could barely move. Her head felt as if it would split. A cloth tied around her mouth made it hard to breathe. "Horus, help me."

The smell of the place was enough to make her nauseous. She was in a cabin that had to be on the pirate ship that had approached the *Horus* yesterday afternoon. She feared for Hui, her attendants and everyone on Pharaoh's ship. She prayed to the gods they were still alive. "They'll use me to get to Father. I should never have left home."

The cabin door flew open. "Well, well. It's one of the false Pharaoh's children."

Unable to respond, Hettie yelled into the cloth and felt her face flush with the effort.

Someone else entered the cabin and stood behind the man she guessed to be the leader. Her eyes grew larger when she recognized Captain Ansra. Why was *he* here? Then she understood. He had betrayed his oath as an officer in Pharaoh's Guards. She had been right to dislike him from the first. To think he had been living in Pharaoh's palace all this time made her more angry.

"We'll untie you if you agree not to leave this cabin," the leader said.

Hettie struggled against her ropes and gag, but finally nodded her head.

The man walked over and untied the cloth from her mouth.

She gasped, and inhaled a great gulp of air.

"Glad you are here, Ansra," the leader said. "Help me untie her hands and feet."

Hettie coughed and shouted, "Touch the royal person and the curse of Horus will be upon you."

The men only laughed as they undid her bonds.

Hettie rubbed her wrists to restore circulation and bent over and rubbed her legs. She looked up and stared at Ansra. She decided to defy them by not speaking another word.

The leader said, "Someone will bring you water and bread. Your personal needs you take care of yourself. Remember, you are our prisoner, not a guest." The two men left and closed the door.

Hettie walked around the cabin to exercise her legs. She opened the window and breathed in fresh air, recognized the smell and looked down. They were back on the sacred river. Hippos bellowed at the ship, while crocodiles simply yawned, annoyed their sleep had been disturbed.

"Where am I? Horus, please let me see a place I recognize."

Hui stood on the ship's deck next to the captain. He rubbed his shoulder where he had fallen on it during the attack. "Where are we now?"

Tiakken said, "We're through the delta and should pass Awen by mid-day. Will we dock, my Lord?"

"Absolutely not. We can't let anyone know what's happened until we reach Memphis."

"There is a problem. We must stop somewhere for food and water."

"Then dock at a village, Captain. We must reach the capital before the assassins. They could send a messenger pigeon to have guards waiting for us. I must be the one who tells Pharaoh what has happened to his daughter, and face the consequence."

"I understand, my Lord."

The first mate interrupted. "This is Senbu, Lord Chamberlain--the guardsman you wanted."

Hui took the man to a more secluded place on deck where they could speak privately. "Tell me what the men are saying. Ansra, their captain, betrayed them, abandoned them in a most traitorous act."

Senbu shook his head and looked Hui in the eye. "They are confused my Lord. Their obedience to Ansra was absolute and they can't understand how an officer could do what he's done."

"And what about his sergeant?"

"His men have tied him up, my Lord. He too is disloyal to us and to Pharaoh. What should we do?"

"You have done the right thing, Guardsman. We'll decide his fate when we land. Right now, I'm concerned about the men. They need someone to command them. As Chamberlain of His Majesty, Pharaoh Khafre, I promote you to Sergeant, Senbu. The men know you and trust you. Tell them we are heading for Memphis as quickly as we can to tell his majesty what has happened. I believe the princess might still be all right. The assassins will hold her for ransom, so we must believe they won't harm her."

"I understand, my Lord."

"What have you done with the bodies of the princess' attendants?"

"We wrapped them in linen sheets, and placed them in the hold. But the men aren't happy. They fear the women's Kas will roam the ship and do evil."

"I do understand, Sergeant. But we must treat them honorably. They died in the service of Pharaoh's daughter. Would it help if I spoke to the men and try to encourage them?"

"It would, my Lord."

"Good. I want them to know you have Pharaoh's authority to command. Keep them busy. Drill them and inspect their weapons—whatever it takes."

"Understood. I know what to do."

On board the pirate ship, the princess stood at the small, open window. She recognized the village of Pa-Osiris as they passed by. It meant they were sailing south toward Memphis.

Her captors brought her a jug of water and a piece of stale bread. They left a tin pail for her personal needs. Her head hurt where they struck her, and a large lump had formed. The leader of the pirates returned once and asked her questions, but she refused to answer.

He scowled at her and left.

Moving away from the window, she sat on the bed. Its linen needed changing and smelled of its previous occupant. She hadn't been able to wash and felt dirty and uncomfortable. She had never really needed to wash herself—her attendants and servants did that. They gave her everything she needed. She swallowed hard as she remembered their bloodied bodies lying on the floor of the royal cabin. She was humiliated having to take care of her body's needs in a pail.

Sleep was impossible. Too many things turned over in her mind. If these men were southerners, the ship could be sailing south beyond Memphis. If it was to Thinis in the old Southern Kingdom, it would be another three-day journey, even a week.

Standing, she walked to the door and tried the handle. It opened! She quickly shut it, but the fact that it opened made her heart jump. Back at the window, she noticed dozens of small canoes bobbing in the ship's wake. Villagers were out fishing and waved to the ship as it passed.

She stuck her head out as far as she could and recognized a marker in the distance. She had seen it many times. They were approaching Giza. The ship was back where this had all begun—the attempted murder of her father beneath the Great Lion. Hurried footsteps on deck told her the ship was slowing down and the crew was pulling the great sail up to its spar. They were docking.

Hui was pleased with how Senbu took command of the guards. Because of his size and physical strength, the men listened to him and jumped at his orders. At the end of each day, he made a report to the chamberlain.

Now, standing on deck again with the ship's captain, Hui realized they were almost home. He still didn't know what to say to Pharaoh. He shared his misgivings with the ship's captain.

Tiakken said, "Tell Pharaoh what you did to protect his daughter, my Lord. Pirates have never attacked one of Pharaoh's ships. There was no way you could have known this would happen." The older mariner paused and ran his fingers through his short-cropped hair. "Haven't you asked yourself how the pirates knew where to find us on the sea? Captain Ansra did that my Lord. Somehow, he sent word to the Phoenician ship and they were just waiting for us. He knew the princess wanted to see the Great Sea. We were like sitting ducks waiting to be bagged."

Hui shook his head in frustration. "I don't know. I think Pharaoh should just kill me and be done with it."This was not his usual reaction to problems, but he knew he could not bear to see the look on Khafre's face when told him his daughter was gone.

Tiakken changed the subject. "We are making good time, my Lord, even against the current. We should arrive by mid-day. Any special instructions?"

"None, Captain. I'll take the guards with me. What you do with his majesty's ship is your concern. You know what to do."

"Very good. But what about the two bodies of her highness's attendants?"

"Forgive me. I completely forgot." Hui paused a moment. "I would recommend you await notice from the palace before moving them to the House of the Dead. I'll send the guards back. If I'm still alive that is."

"Yes, my Lord. I remember how superstitious the crew can be with the dead onboard."

Hui nodded. "I understand. Why not take the deceased to one of the storage warehouses, at least to calm your men."

"Very well. I'll do as you say."

Hui walked forward to the bow to admire the passing countryside. Children onshore waved to him and he smiled. Village life was so much more simple and natural. For a moment, he envied them. And then, the white walls of Memphis appeared around the bend and his heartbeat quickened. Soon, it would all be over. He would either be dead or in prison.

"Tie her hands," Ansra ordered one of his men. "You, woman, can either agree to not cry out, or be knocked out again. Personally, I prefer the latter."

Hettie didn't reply and Ansra left. When he returned, he said, "Put this on." He held out a soiled, smelly robe.

She waited for him to leave before changing. She assumed they didn't want people to recognize her. No one would look twice at a common villager leaving the ship.

She turned up her nose at the smell of it, but had no other choice.

When Ansra returned, he led her out on deck. "Follow me. Look straight ahead." With the walkway lowered, Ansra headed down to a waiting wagon. "Get in," he ordered. He didn't offer her his hand as he should, so she stepped up onto a fragile plank and sat next to several sacks of grain.

Directly in front of them lay the Great Lion and the Pyramid behind it. Why here, she wondered? What purpose could there be to bring her here to the burial place of her grandfather Khufu?

The horses pulled away and they followed an old road that led out into the desert. Ansra and two other men sat on the seat in front. One of them turned around and tied a cloth over her eyes.

"Don't take it off," the man growled.

Hettie panicked. She was trying to remember the road, but now she could only see a little from the bottom of the blindfold, and it was all sand.

"He's going to be pleased," Ansra said. "He didn't think we'd be able to do it, but the spirit of our great Pharaoh helped us."

She knew he meant Djedefre and not her father. Hui was right. These men were part of the band still loyal to her uncle. Without doubt, they would kill her once they drew the king away from the palace.

The team of horses pulled the wagon for what seemed a very long way from the river. They stopped and removed her blindfold. When her eyes adjusted to the light, she found they were at a large outcropping of stone. It resembled the side of a mountain, sliced with a sword and stuck into the sand. She smiled, because she knew where she was.

She and her father would often ride up here when she was little. Khafre called it the place of the Lizard's Tail, because the rocks looked like the end of the reptile's appendage. They were perhaps only five miles from the Great Pyramid.

"Get down," Ansra ordered.

She climbed down and he gripped her roughly and pushed her ahead. She couldn't see their destination, until they stopped at a large opening in the cliff. It had to be a cave. The princess had a deadly fear of such places. Her older brother left her once up in the hills outside Memphis. She cried for the longest time until her father found her.

"In here," Ansra growled. "Tie her hands. Undo them only to let her eat."

One of the other men took rope from the wagon and tied her hands in front of her this time, and pulled them so tight she cried out.

"You two remain with her," Ansra said. "I'll ride back and meet with our leader."

The men grumbled, but nodded in agreement.

Ansra untied one of the horses from the wagon, and rode back toward the river.

Hettie trembled from the tension of the ordeal and hoped it would soon be over. She sat on a wooden box and tears streamed down her cheeks. "Help me, Horus. Don't let me die."

CHAPTER SIXTEEN

General Herihor walked toward the royal Hall of Audiences. His scouts had spotted the Princess's ship approaching Memphis and he wanted to be the one to tell his majesty of her arrival. He already knew that the royal daughter was not onboard.

Lord Rabiah, the king's very old friend, was the acting chamberlain and he announced the general's arrival.

Herihor stood at attention, waiting for the king to raise his hand. However, his majesty was intent on his conversation with the queen and hadn't heard the announcement.

Lord Rabiah hesitated to offend the king by striking the floor again with his staff. Both men stood there until their majesties concluded their conversation.

"Majesty," Rabiah said again, "General Herihor."

The king raised his hand and the general advanced. "We are pleased to see you, Lord General. What brings you to us?"

"I bring you joy, Majesties. Princess Rekhetre's ship has passed the point. She should be here by mid-afternoon."

"Hettie," Queen Persenet exclaimed.

"Thank you, my Lord," Pharaoh said. "It is good news indeed."

"Captain Ansra is with her. I will send several brigades of my men to welcome her back, Majesty."

Khafre nodded. "Excellent, General. See to it."

The warrior saluted, fist to the chest. "Majesty," he said. He bowed his head, did an about face and followed Lord Rabiah out of the hall.

Pharaoh turned to his wife. "Why is he so pleased? He usually looks like a horse with a toothache."

His wife laughed and nodded her head.

Khafre frowned. "We know he doesn't like the royal family. Why make a deliberate attempt to please us? It's out of character."

"But you'll go to meet her anyway, Husband."

"Yes, beloved. She'll expect me there." He called for the acting captain of the Guard and told him he would be going to greet the ship. The officer ordered his majesty's chariot, and the guards who would march with the king to the landing.

Word quickly spread through the capital that the princess was returning and crowds began to assemble on the dock. The army moved into place, lining the streets for Pharaoh's arrival.

"I want to come with you, Father," Prince Duaenre said.

"Excellent," Khafre replied. "Tell the guards to prepare your chariot."

Father and son watched for the ship from the veranda. From their vantage point, they could see when the ship reached the bend of the river nearest the city. When they spotted it, they walked down the steps in front of the palace and stepped into their chariots.

The royal guards marched in front of and behind the king and the prince. Another brigade ran on each side of them. Crowds cheered their names and clapped as they passed. Young girls threw flowers at the prince and he waved and smiled.

The ship completed its docking, and the guardsmen stood at attention. Captain Tiakken and the lord chamberlain stood at the top of the walkway—waiting to welcome them.

Hui stood immobile, his eyes fixed directly on the approaching procession, his face as stiff as granite. It hid the inner turmoil of his Ka.

"We must go down to greet him, my Lord," Tiakken said.

"I know, Captain. I just can't get my legs to move."

Tiakken chuckled and pushed Hui ahead of him down the steps. They waited at the top of the walkway while the crew lined up on deck hoping for a glimpse of the living god of Egypt.

Princess Hettie's ship flew the long royal banners from the rigging, and flashes of blue and yellow floated majestically in the wind. Army drummers beat loudly as the two chariots approached the blue carpet laid out for them.

Trumpeters blew a long fanfare as Pharaoh reined in his horses, and then stepped out of his chariot. Prince Dua stopped behind him and followed his father up the carpet.

Hui spoke in his loudest voice, "Hail, Khafre! Pharaoh of Upper and Lower Egypt. Son of Ra, and beloved of the gods. Hail Duaenre, Crown Prince and son of Pharaoh, blessed of Horus!"

Khafre stepped on deck and as soon as his feet touched it, Captain Tiakken fell prostrate before the king, as did the crowd, the crew and the Lord Chamberlain.

Pharaoh raised his hand, the signal that everyone could stand. He slowly looked around. "Where is she, Hui? Is she unwell?"

"Come with me, Majesty," Hui said.

Khafre and the prince followed him up the steps to the royal cabin. Hui opened the door and the king and his son went inside.

"What is this, Hui?" Khafre's voice grew louder. "Where is Hettie?"

"She's been captured, Majesty. We don't know where she is."

Pharaoh's face turned red. He grabbed Hui and placed both hands on the chamberlain's throat. "How could you?" he shouted. When Hui began to gasp, he pushed him onto the floor and stormed out of the cabin. He stood at the railing and shouted, "Captain Nuru!"

The army officer ran up the walkway and saluted. "Majesty?"

"Arrest the Chamberlain, and all of the royal guards who were on this ship, immediately!"

The captain turned and shouted to his men on the dock. Two soldiers hurried up and boarded the ship. They stood at attention until the chamberlain came down.

Hui handed Iset to Prince Dua. “Take care of her.”

Pharaoh turned away from him, and Hui walked down the steps and waited while the two soldiers led him by the arms down to the dock. He knew it was futile to try to tell the king what happened. He looked back, and took courage when he saw Pharaoh summon Captain Tiakken to his side.

The guards escorted Hui up the road toward the king’s prison. He cringed when Pharaoh and the prince raced past them on their chariots, leaving them in a cloud of dust. Through the noise, Iset’s fearful wailing rose above the sound of the racing horses and broke his heart.

Prince Dua’s right arm was bleeding. Iset had dug her claws into it trying to hang on as his chariot raced back to the palace.

“She didn’t mean it, Mother,” he told the queen. “She was afraid of the chariot. I should have known better.”

Queen Persenet used a basin of water and linen cloth to wipe away the dust and blood. “Her scratches aren’t deep, Dua. You’ll be fine. I’ll put ointment on them.” When she finished, her son kissed her and walked toward the living room.

His father paced back and forth, pulling on his goatee.

“It was not his fault, Father. How can you punish him?”

“Quiet, squealing toad! He vowed to protect your sister, and he failed. Are you not angry that she is gone?”

Dua nodded. "She is annoying at times, but I will miss her if they kill her."

That disturbed the king. "Dua! Do not even think that. If these pirates, or whoever they are, have her, they will ask for a ransom. You will see."

Iset tip-toed in and approached the king. She meowed and rubbed against Pharaoh's shins. Then she recognized Dua and headed for him. He picked her up and she purred loudly.

"It looks like she has forgiven your chariot driving, my Son."

"I think so."

"Meowrell..."

"She misses Hui. Can I take her to visit him?"

"It is not proper for the Crown Prince of Egypt to visit a lowly prisoner. It would not be very royal or dignified."

"But I thought he was family, Father."

"When you said 'was,' you spoke the truth. I cannot pardon what he has done."

"But I still want to go."

"I will hear no more about it."

Dua waited a moment and said, "We must send troops out to find her."

"I am giving that some thought. I will have General Herihor send out patrols up and down the river. If the Band of Djed are behind this, they will pay."

"Good, and Horus will help us," Dua said.

"If he wills, Son."

Dua left holding Iset in his arms. In his room, he put her down on his bed. "Wait here, Iset. I will be back." He went to the door connecting to the hallway, and called one of the guards.

"You will go to the prison with me. I want to speak with the chamberlain."

"Does your father agree, Highness?"

"It is not your concern. Do as I say."

"Yes, my Lord. When will you go?"

"Now. First, I need Iset." He hurried back inside and returned with her on his shoulder.

The guard led him down the corridor to the outside. The prison was at the bottom of the hill, a quarter of a mile away. They passed through the outer gates and the sergeant in charge of the prison took them to Hui's cell.

"Unlock it," Dua ordered, and when it was open, he went in.

Hui started to prostrate himself, but Dua stopped him.

Iset jumped down from Dua's shoulder and ran over to the prisoner. Hui embraced the cat and laughed as she nuzzled him and meowed happily.

"Thank you, Highness for bringing her here, but she's not safe. You will take her back with you I pray."

"Yes, of course, Hui."

"I regret I have no chair for you, Prince."

"No matter. Please tell me about my sister."

"Very well," Hui began. He told him about their visit to Awen and finished with the attack at sea. "That's all I remember because the pirates knocked me out."

Iset rubbed her cheek against his head. "Meoooww…"

Hui continued. "When I awoke, I found her two attendants dead, and your sister gone. They drugged the crew and guards and escaped in the night. I still have the lump on my head."

"The curse of Seth fall on them!" Dua swore.

"Agreed."

"Father will have to forgive you when he hears your story."

"He'll not listen to me, my Prince. He's too angry and he has every right to throw me in prison or even execute me. He is Pharaoh."

"Hmm," Dua said. "He will change his mind. He will find out how loyal you are, Cousin. I will send one of the guards back with some food for you tonight."

"Thank you, Prince. I feel bad for the guards and the ship's crew. Captain Ansra drugged them all. There was nothing they could have done."

"I understand," Dua said. "May Horus be with you, Chamberlain."

"And with you, Great Prince."

Dua and the guard walked back with Iset and returned to his room.

"What can we do, Iset? Hui needs to help Father find Hettie and he cannot do that from prison."

"Mowerrr…?" Iset jumped up on the room's window sill and mewed again. She looked toward the prince and cried out once more.

"What is it?" Dua asked. He stood and walked to the window, but couldn't see anything out of the ordinary.

"Meow…" Iset cried again. She nudged him and sat looking down at the river.

"What?" Dua said. "Wait! The ship! You are looking at the ship. Of course! Thank you, cat!" He hugged her and went back into the hallway. He called the guard back over to him.

"Bring the Captain of the princess's ship."

"Yes, Highness," the guard said.

Dua walked into the living room to find his father, but the steward said his majesty had gone out and he didn't know where.

Shortly after, the guard returned. "The Captain is not on the ship, Highness. He's in prison with the rest of his crew. I'm sorry, Prince, I didn't know either." He saluted and left.

Back in the prince's room, Iset hid in the basket she had used on the ship. A servant had brought it to the prince's room along with her collar and leash.

"Why are you hiding in that old thing, cat?" Dua asked.

"Meowol…owl…" she replied. Climbing out, she walked over to him. She deposited something from her mouth on the floor in front of him.

Dua stooped down and picked it up. He dried it off and examined it closely. "What is it?"

"Mufffrrr..."

It was a small piece of leather. Dua turned it over and saw a mark on it. Taking it closer to the window, the sunlight made it easier to see, but it was not familiar to him.

"Oh well, we'll show it to Hui. He'll know what it is." He picked her up and rubbed behind her ears. She purred and looked up at his face, patting his chin with her paw.

"So you are happy now, is that it? Good." He paused and then said, "I have an idea. We will take Hui some food. Who knows, in the kitchen we might find something you like too."

After the cook gave him some bread, goat cheese, fresh dates and a little jar of honey, the prince and Iset walked back with a guard to the prison. This time, however, the guard refused to let them in.

"Sorry, Highness. His Majesty's orders," the guard said.

"What? But I was here earlier today. Let me in. That's an order."

The inside door opened and a stern voice said, "You have done well, Guardsman."

Dua swallowed hard. It was his father's voice. "Majesty," he said.

The guard opened the door and let the prince in.

"You disobeyed me young man," Pharaoh said.

"But..."

"Follow me."

Dua walked behind him, down to Hui's cell. Inside were the captain of the ship and a guardsman Dua didn't recognize.

"What is going on," the prince asked.

Pharaoh entered the cell and said, "Captain Tiakken has told me what really happened to your sister, and Sergeant Senbu has corroborated it all. I've come to set him and the ship's company free."

"Oh," was all Dua could say. "I've brought your food, Lord Chamberlain."

"So, stealing from the kitchen too? Is there no end of your crimes?" Pharaoh asked. "Let us return to the palace. We have much to discuss," He turned, and led the way out.

Dua said, "I think you've done the 'royal' thing, Father. That is, a royal person humbling himself to enter a prison."

"Humph!" Pharaoh grumbled.

Captain Tiakken said, "Thank you for releasing the crew, Majesty."

"My friend, Pharaoh cannot make a mistake. Let us just say, they were guests of the king overnight."

Dua smiled. His father was right. One never corrected Pharaoh. Horus spoke through him and the gods could not make mistakes.

When they were back in the palace, Hui and Tiakken washed up in the servant's room off the royal apartment before entering Pharaoh's living room.

Dua walked to his room and returned with Iset's treasure.

"Iset had this in her basket, Hui. Do you know what it is?"

Hui examined it and shook his head.

"What is it?" Pharaoh asked. "Let me see it."

Hui handed him the small piece of leather.

Khafre examined it then turned it over. "By the gods! I know this. Where did she get it?"

"On the ship, Majesty," Hui said. "It's the only place she's been with her basket."

Pharaoh swore, "By Seth's foul stench! This is General Herihor's mark. I know it well." He clenched his fists and growled, "I can't wait to get my hands on him!"

CHAPTER SEVENTEEN

Hettie ached all over. Every muscle hurt. Sleeping on the floor of a cave was something she had never experienced before—ever. Sitting up, she stretched her arms, then her long legs. She was tall and needed to move about. There were indentions on her arms and legs from small stones. Her hair felt like thick ropes, encrusted with an accumulation of dust.

Her captors brought her food and water twice a day. The stale bread and dried dates didn't agree with her and made her sick. Surprisingly, her captors also left her untied. If she tried to escape, she wouldn't survive this far out in the desert. She couldn't run away in the night. There were too many jackals and hyenas eager to make a meal of her. The men kept their distance to avoid any attempt by her to steal a weapon or horse.

The hardest part she found was not being able to speak to anyone. To keep her wits, she would talk aloud—if for nothing else, to hear a human voice.

Captain Ansra came each morning, but didn't stay long. On the second morning, he had a satisfied look on his face.

"Your father, the usurper, has learned you were not aboard your ship when it docked. Now he will feel the wrath of the Band of Djed! Tomorrow, your life will come to an end."

Hettie crossed her arms and scowled. She wouldn't respond, and turned her back on him. She wasn't afraid of him. What she did fear, however, was the nights. Instead of sleeping, she threw stones at vipers and lizards. Bats flew in early in the morning and out again at night. The odor of their guano filled the cave, and she slept near the entrance to breathe fresh air.

The robe given her on the ship smelled worse than it did when she first put it on. When she asked for a pail of water, the men refused. If her family saw her now, they would recoil in horror. She thought she might never see them again and wept until tears ran down her cheeks. There were no sobs, only tears she couldn't stop.

Hettie regretted not having spent enough time with her mother. How often had the queen tried to make time for them to be together? Hettie always shrugged it off and her brother was like a stranger now that he was becoming a man.

"Oh, Horus," she prayed. "Bring us together again. I will offer sacrifices to honor you the rest of my days."

"Who are you talking to in there?" one of the captors yelled. "Keep it down."

The other laughed. "Maybe her dead Captain Paru has come back to haunt her." That provoked more laughter which echoed in the cave. Hettie covered her ears.

Most of all, Hettie regretted losing a love she thought would last. This band of assassins killed Paru and there would be no more love for her in the future. She couldn't trust her father's judgment in choosing a husband. Why couldn't he find someone like Hui? He was a friend, confidant, and she thought he was genuinely fond of her. He often used his cat as an excuse just to see her. The strange thing was it was working. She looked forward to his visits, and so did her family.

As the sun reached its highest point, she moved her blanket further into the shadows of the cave. She wiped away the sweat with the dirty sleeve of her robe and regretted how many times she had chastised her handmaidens for wiping her brow too roughly. What she wouldn't give for a few moments in her glorious copper tub filled with warm water and bath oils.

When she spread the blanket on the ground, something bit her hand. She cried out in pain and ran outside. Whatever it was, it slithered back into the shadows.

"Help! A snake's bitten me. Do something! Don't let me die!"

Her guards rushed to her side and examined the bite on her hand.

"Get her on the horse," the taller one said.

"Put your foot in the stirrup," the other ordered.

She did so, threw her leg over and settled into the saddle.

The two men got on the other horse together and held Hettie's reins. They urged their horse into a gallop and Hettie's mount followed.

The princess's hand began to throb and she saw it was turning red. She knew if it was a viper, she would be dead before they reached the road leading into Giza. "Hurry!" she shouted. "I'm feeling dizzy."

The men dug their heels into the horse's flanks and galloped faster.

As Hettie's horse sped up, she leaned forward and held onto its neck and mane.

Reaching the market of Giza, they asked directions to the physician's surgery. When they found it, they reined in their horses at the house of the only healer in the region.

Dismounting, the older thug said, "No talking. Only shake your head if he asks you a question. We'll say you can't speak."

Before they opened the door, the other whispered, “If you tell him who you are, we’ll be forced to kill him and his death will be on you.”

Once inside, a white-haired gentleman greeted them. “I am Lord Psammis, what is the problem?”

The room was clean, but basic. There were no fancy tiles or paintings to cheer up the place. The strong fragrance of cloves and other medicines permeated the waiting room.

Hettie’s captors told Psammis that a snake had bitten her.

“Was it a viper?” the healer asked, and then grimaced. “Of course not. If it had been, she would have been dead before you got here. Was it a cobra?”

Hettie shrugged her shoulders.

“Well, what kind was it?” the physician asked again.

“She didn’t see it, my Lord—she only felt the bite,” the first man answered.

“Very well.” He washed the wound with clean water, and examined the puncture marks closely. “There’s no swelling. That’s a good sign.” Rubbing some ointment on the wound, he used a linen strip to wrap around it, tying it tightly.

Hettie suddenly had an inspiration. She turned her head to the left, hoping Lord Psammis would see her royal mark. All of Pharaoh’s children received the mark a small falcon at the base of the neck. Only the royal family could use the sacred sign.

When Psammis finished tying the bandage, she sighed a breath of relief when she saw him look at the back of her leaned toward him as if she were dizzy. Psammis's large when he saw the falcon. Their eyes met and he waited until the two men weren't looking and nodded his head.

"I'm finished here," he said. "Bring her back if she gets a fever or her hand swells. Here's some powder to help her sleep. That'll be one copper."

The older of the two paid, and the two men led Hettie back to the horse. She was about to get on when she felt very dizzy and collapsed on the ground.

One of the men ran back into the surgery and yelled for the physician. "She's collapsed, my Lord. Hurry!"

Lord Psammis rushed out and felt Hettie's pulse. "Carry her back in. The venom is making her lose consciousness. I'll need to watch her until she comes to—if she does that is."

"We'll sit in the waiting room, my Lord. Tell us if there is any change. She is very important to our master. See that you keep her alive or else."

"I understand," Psammis said. "Now I must stay with her."

The two men sat in the room while the physician returned to his examining room. Hettie lay on the table, but as soon as he drew back the curtain, she opened her eyes and sat up.

The physician whispered. "Forgive me, Highness. A thousand pardons. I didn't know until I saw the falcon."

"Shh. Listen, my Lord. These assassins captured me and brought me here. I must get word to Pharaoh that I'm alive and in a cave of the Lizard's Tail near Giza."

"I can be your messenger, but will his Majesty believe me, Princess?"

"He will. He knows I'm missing. He needs to know I'm alive. Now, is my bite fatal?"

"Not at all, Highness. It was a probably a desert egg-eater. They only bite to defend themselves. They are not known to kill humans."

"Hurry up in there," one of the captor's shouted.

"Coming" the physician yelled back.

"Wait," Hettie whispered. "Tell Father to take care of Iset. Remember those words. It will prove you've seen me."

"Yes, Highness. May Horus protect us."

She nodded, and got down off the examining table.

"Pretend to be ill, my Lady. Act dizzy, nauseous. It might help prolong your life."

"I will." She opened the door and slowed her steps as she walked to her horse. A new spirit of hope strengthened her resolve to survive.

Pharaoh paced back and forth in the palace. His son, Hui and sergeant Pubu sat watching him.

"I somehow knew Herihor would be behind all this," Khafre said. "Captain Ansra must have dropped this piece of leather, or it fell off one of their band when they boarded the ship. It means the general and he are working together."

Hui said, “As a commander of the army Herihor would know the royal family’s schedule for any voyages they might make. He would have eyes everywhere.” He paused a moment. “What I can’t understand is how Captain Ansra could be such a good guardsman and be so disloyal to his Pharaoh.” He turned to the sergeant. “What about it, Pubu?”

The guardsman’s face flushed and he found it difficult to speak. “I can’t explain it either, my Lord. Honor and respect for Pharaoh is first in everything we do—why else be in the guards? I chose them because of what Pharaoh Khufu—of respected memory—did for me. During a severe drought one year, your father, Majesty, sent the guards to help dig a well for my village situated on the edge of the desert. That water saved our crops and lives. All of the Guards have similar stories. I cannot imagine why Ansra joined.”

“Well spoken,” Pharaoh said. “It’s what I thought all men in the Guards believed.”

“It makes what Ansra did even more insidious,” Hui growled.

Prince Dua asked, “But why have the assassins not asked for a ransom, Father? Does that mean Hettie’s dead?”

“No, Son. I believe she’s alive. They just have not told us what they want. Once they do, we will decide how to respond.”

Lord Psammis approached the gate leading to the royal palace to give Pharaoh Hettie's message. He had to stop to catch his breath. Once the princess left his surgery, he became anxious about delivering it. What if someone followed him? Would he be able to get past the guards? He thought he had a solid reason for them letting him in, but was still nervous about using it.

A guard approached him and the physician swallowed hard. Sweat covered his brow as he waited for the guard's question. "What is your business here?"

"I must see Pharaoh's physician," Psammis said.

The guard recognized the robe the man wore as that of a physician. "Wait here. I'll check with the commander."

Psammis waited patiently, unsure if he should have used another story.

"You may enter, my Lord," the guard said.

Psammis passed through the gate and the guard pointed him in the direction of the apartment of Pharaoh's physician. When he reached the door, a servant opened it.

"Can I help you, my Lord?"

"I am Psammis, physician of Giza. I have important news for the royal physician."

"Lord Anebos is somewhere in the palace, my Lord. You may wait in the garden."

"Very well. Could I have some water?"

"Of course. I'll bring some right away."

Psammis walked into the formal garden and chose to sit on a bench beneath a date palm. In the small pool, golden fish swam to the surface hoping to catch a careless fly. It was a long time until approaching footsteps signaled the physician's arrival.

"How may I help you, my Lord?" a large and very corpulent man said walking toward him.

"I am Psammis, my Lord, physician at Giza. I must give a message to his majesty. I was hoping you might take me to him. I know of no other way."

The royal physician nodded. "I see. I am Anebos, and have been his majesty's healer these ten summers. How do I know you are *what* you say you are, that is, a physician? Anyone could have stolen that robe."

Psammis sighed, and then frowned. He didn't anticipate anyone questioning his word. He quickly told the nobleman the types of patients he treated and their cures.

"Excellent, my Lord. It is always good to meet a colleague."

"I agree, my Lord. Now can we go to his majesty?"

"Yes, of course." Anebos stood and started back up the path to his home. "Can you share with me what makes this message so urgent? After all, you could be coming to kill my master."

Psammis thought for a moment, and then decided to tell him. "Princess Rekhetre has been found, my Lord. Pharaoh must be told."

"That's good news indeed. We must go through my house to reach the hallway connecting to the royal apartments.

"Very well," Psammis said.

Abruptly without warning, the royal physician struck Psammis on the side of the head.

Dazed, he fell to the floor. Anebos fell on top of him and tried to strangle him. The weight of such a heavy man knocked the breath out of Psammis. He managed to push him off and struck the physician on the jaw with his fist, knocking him out.

The servant rushed in. "What's happened?"

"Your master's fallen. Help me get him up."

It took all their strength to move the big man onto a divan in the front room.

"Show me to the surgery," Psammis ordered.

"This way my Lord."

Inside the surgery, Psammis said, "Return and stay with your master. I must find the right medication."

The servant nodded and returned to his master.

Psammis looked quickly around at all the jars and pots and found the powder he wanted. Returning, he asked the servant for a cup of wine. He then mixed a lethal dose of the powder into the cup.

"Stay with him. He'll have a very bad headache when he wakens. Give him this wine. It will help relieve the pain. Now show me the connecting passage."

"Just follow this hallway to the blue door, my Lord."

Psammis followed the hall to the door and opened it. He stepped out into the corridor and followed it to Pharaoh's residence. He told one of the guards who he was and that Lord Anebos had sent him to Pharaoh.

Pharaoh and his friends had finished discussing what they would do when a demand for a ransom arrived. His steward entered and interrupted them.

"Forgive, Majesty. But there is a physician here with an urgent message."

"Oh? I didn't ask for any physician. Send him away."

Hui spoke up. He felt compelled to ask, "Where is he from?"

The servant nodded and returned a short time later and said, "He's from Giza."

"Giza!" Khafre exclaimed. "Bring him in."

When the man entered, he looked surprised to find other people in the room. He made obeisance to Pharaoh on the floor and Khafre raised his hand.

"Stand, my Lord Physician, what is it?"

"I have a message from your daughter, Majesty."

Khafre's face lit up. "Hettie? What is it?"

"First, Great Pharaoh, she told me to say these words. They are very important. 'Tell Father to take care of Iset.' Does that make sense?"

Dua and Khafre laughed and Hui joined in.

"Yes, only Hettie would know we would accept the message about Hui's cat."

"She is well, Great One. I treated her in my surgery in Giza for a harmless snake bite. She's being held by assassins in the desert. She wanted you to know she is still alive."

Pharaoh stood and approached the man. "We are grateful—my family and I, for this message, Lord Healer." He broke all custom and laws by placing his hand on the man's shoulder.

Khafre turned to his son, "Dua, go and tell your mother that we have learned that Hettie is alive and well."

"Yes, Father." The prince quickly left the room.

Abruptly, Psammis threw himself on the floor again. "Mercy, Pharaoh, I must beg forgiveness."

"Stand up, man," Pharaoh said. "What is it?"

"Majesty, I fear I have killed your physician. He tried to stop me and struck me once he learned what the message was. I made a poisoned wine for him to drink when he comes to. The servant will give it to him. Oh, Majesty, I have done wrong."

"Gods!" Khafre exclaimed. "Even my personal physician is a traitor. They are everywhere in my kingdom!"

Hui said, "Let's go first and see if he is dead, Majesty. If not, we can perhaps learn who is behind all of these attacks."

"Agreed. Come with us, physician," Pharaoh said.

Hui, Dua and Pubu followed Pharaoh and Lord Psammis down the corridor to the royal physician's house. They entered just as the steward was giving Lord Anebos the drink Psammis prepared for him.

"Stop!" Pharaoh shouted.

The steward fell face down on the floor.

Lord Anebos coughed and got up and bowed to Pharaoh. "Majesty, this is a surprise. What is wrong?" Abruptly he had trouble swallowing and gasped for air.

Pharaoh scowled. "Tell me, who paid you to betray your king, Anebos? You have swallowed a poison and the wrath of the gods will end your life." He grabbed the fat man's shoulder. "Tell me."

Only gurgling came from the physician's mouth which formed into a sinister grin. He stuttered, "D-d-d-d. . ." and breathed his last.

"Gods!" Khafre said. "Djedfre again! Curse him!

Hui wasn't certain if his majesty meant to curse the physician or his brother.

"Take him out of my sight," Pharaoh said.

Sergeant Pubu left at once to find men to carry out the dead healer.

Pharaoh grabbed Hui's arm. "Come, Hui. Let us devise a plan if this band of devils send a ransom note."

CHAPTER EIGHTEEN

An ordinary fisherman brought the ransom note the next day. The guards took him to the chamberlain's office.

The elderly man, his clothes tattered and smelling of the day's catch, said, "It's for his majesty."

Hui gave him a copper coin. "Thank you, friend. We are grateful. I will take it to Pharaoh at once. Who gave it to you?"

"He was a general, my Lord. I could tell by his uniform. He gave me a silver coin to deliver it."

"I see. Thank you again. A guard will show you out."

The man nodded, and left.

Hui unrolled the unsealed papyrus and read the message:

> In 2 nights, when Khonsu is overhead,
> the Usurper, Khafre, will stand as
> ransom for his daughter in the temple
> of the Great Lion.
>
> Djedefre Lives.

Iset jumped up on Hui's desk and sniffed at the papyrus, attracted to the fishy smell. "Meowwwrrr…?"

"I agree, Iset. Pharaoh's definitely not going to be happy."

She followed him to the Hall of Audiences, but Khafre wasn't there. Hui decided to look for him in the formal dressing room.

Hui entered and said, "It's here, Majesty." He handed the papyrus scroll to the king. "It was unsealed."

After reading the message, Khafre shouted, "By Seth's unholy name! What kind of ransom demand is this?"

"They are very clear, Great One. They want you, not your daughter nor any gold."

"Gods," the king swore. "Get this off me!" His attendants rushed to remove the double crown from his head. "Cancel all petitioners, and call General Haka, Sergeant Pubu and Captain Basa, the new commander of the Guard."

"Yes, Majesty. Shall we meet at mid-morning?"

"Agreed. I'll bring Prince Duaenre."

Later, with everyone assembled in the king's council chamber, his majesty entered with his son. Dua carried Iset in his arms. At first Hui thought it was her. The cat jumped down onto the table and headed right for Hui. It sniffed him, then jumped onto his shoulder and sniffed his head and ears.

"Meorrrr..." it said.

Hui was astonished. The cat looked just like Iset—the same colored markings and short hair—except it was male. "Who is this, Lord Prince?"

"This is Khensu. He runs as fast as the wind. I miss Iset when she's with you, Hui. I wanted a cat of my own. He acts so much like her."

"Forget cats!" Pharaoh exclaimed. "Let us talk about how to rescue my daughter. We only have two nights to find an answer."

General Haka said, "You must not go to Giza, Majesty. Let your army sail there, unload the men and horses a mile before the causeway. We can circle around behind the pyramid and hide close to the new temple. We'll kill the band of Djed when they try to enter it."

Khafre shook his head. "No, no. The princess is our priority. You must rescue her before I enter the temple. This is all about my daughter, nothing more."

Hui could hear the concern in Pharaoh's voice. "And we agree, Pharaoh. I think what the general is saying is that we can do both. Under the cover of darkness, you can wait outside the temple, and they will let Hettie come out first. You will wear your brass breastplate and helmet which look like gold. They are so strong, no arrow can pierce them."

Haka nodded. "I agree, Lord Hui. As precious as the princess is to us all, Majesty, you are Pharaoh. Your people need you. Don't risk your life, I pray you."

Khafre paused a moment. "You have spoken well, General, and you are right. Egypt must come first even before Pharaoh. But I fear we will lose the element of surprise with this plan."

Hui said, "I have been asking questions, my Lords. Why did they choose the Great Lion for this exchange? Why not a place where they would have the advantage?"

Khafre frowned. "Is it because they failed the last time when they shot you instead of me? I can't explain it." He paused awhile and then added, "Perhaps it's because my brother repaired the temple and parts of the Great Lion. That project is something we both wanted to complete in order to honor our father, Khufu, of blessed memory."

Hui nodded. "There is another problem, Majesty. I've been to the monuments several times. There are no places for our soldiers to hide. There is a small back room behind the altar which couldn't hide more than twenty men."

The king nodded. "You are right. Let us study the problem and return this evening at sunset."

Everyone agreed.

As Hui was about to leave the room, Prince Dua said, "May I go home with you, Lord Chamberlain? I would like to introduce Khensu to Iset. I hope they can be friends."

"Of course, Highness. I will be interested to see if she even recognizes his existence. She's very particular about who she chooses to adopt."

At the villa, Hui's steward opened the door and the enticing aroma of his housekeeper's cooking filled the house.

"Let me go in first. I want to be holding Iset when you bring him in."

The prince nodded and closed the door again.

"Meowwww..." Iset said, running to greet him. He picked her up, hugged her and she purred like a small drum. He nodded to the steward to open the door for the prince.

When Iset saw him, her ears perked up and her nose sniffed the air.

Hui said, "We welcome you, Highness. Please make yourself comfortable."

Dua walked to one of the divans and held his cat in his arms waiting to see how Iset would react.

Hui let her go and she looked at him with her gorgeous eyes. "Merreeowww...?"

"Go see who is here, Iset," Hui said. "Who is it?" He nodded to the prince. "Let him go, Highness. We have to see what will happen."

Dua let Khensu loose and the cat got down and sat on the floor as still as a statue. He watched every move Iset made.

She paced around the room, and then stopped in front of the prince.

"Meowlll?..."

"Hello, Iset," Dua said. "This is Khensu, son of the goddess Bastet, and a god of the air. He wants to be your friend."

Iset hissed, growled and then turned up her nose.

Khensu growled back, strutted around and then followed her.

Iset abruptly turned back, sat down and began to wash her face. Khensu walked around her, careful not to get too close. She ignored him and he finally sat facing her, his tail curled up around him.

"I don't believe it," Hui said. "She's ignoring him."

Then to their surprise, Khensu walked over to Iset and rubbed his cheek against hers. She purred as they began to groom each other.

"Whew," Hui said. "You'd think they had known each other for years."

"I'm relieved," Dua said. "I love Iset, and I didn't want him to harm her. Bastet the cat goddess is to be praised."

"Even so," Hui said. "Will you take the mid-day meal with me, Highness, before we return to the palace? By the wonderful aroma, Kebi has prepared roast beef."

"I am so worried about my sister and my father's fate I can't think of food. But out of courtesy, I will make an attempt to eat."

Hui couldn't help smiling. "Good, come along." The two men took their places at the table, and enjoyed a nourishing meal of roast beef, cabbage and other steamed vegetables. Kebi's fresh bread with wild honey, added to their enjoyment. For dessert, she served plump yellow pears.

During the meal, the two men ignored their cats and discussed how best to rescue the princess and keep Pharaoh safe.

When they returned to the front room, Dua said, "You are not pleased with the general's plan, are you?"

"I don't understand it. I'm torn between your father and sister. Hettie is in greater danger. She's being held by them somewhere in the desert. Only the gods know what she is suffering."

"Well, I was thinking while we were at the meeting, if we could find where they're hiding her—and it can't be far from the pyramid—we could attack that group first and take her out of danger. Their main band will be waiting for Pharaoh near the temple of the Great Lion."

Hui nodded. "An excellent suggestion. General Haka should know what kind of settlements or hiding places are near the Giza plateau."

"Meow..." Iset interrupted. She and Khensu walked into the front room and settled on the men's laps. Each feline rubbed its head against the men's chests, hoping to be petted.

"Can I leave Khensu here tonight? They could get to know each other better."

"Well," Hui hesitated, "how much better do we want them to get along, Cousin? A litter of kittens?"

Dua laughed. "I never thought of that."

General Haka reported back to the king at the evening meeting. "The Lord Chamberlain requests information on the locations of hiding places near the Great Pyramid, Majesty."

Khafre nodded. "And what have you found?"

"The physician said Hettie identified the cave as the one at the Lizard's Tail. That has to be it. My men believe they are keeping the princess there. There are no other places. There's water at the cave, and it is the perfect hiding place."

Khafre smiled. "I know the place. There are several caves there."

Hui said, "This is good news, General. The physician said they were keeping her in the desert, but not far. What do you propose?"

The general said, "I say we surprise them, Majesty. Send in a group of our best warriors tonight. They could sail for Giza immediately, land and ride around behind the monuments and follow the merchant's trail. Using our best archers, the first group will pick off the princess's guards and retrieve her."

"This is not a retrieval!" Khafre shouted. "It is a rescue."

"Forgive my unfortunate choice of words, Great One," Haka said.

"Assure the men who rescue her, that they will be well-rewarded. Go now, and may Horus go with you."

"In Pharaoh's name," the others shouted.

Hettie believed she was going mad. The heat, bats, snakes and other creatures kept her from sleeping. She was completely exhausted.

When she removed the physician's bandage from her hand, the redness was gone, and there was no scar. She couldn't even find the snake's puncture marks.

Her guards finally left her a pail of water which enabled her to bathe, then wash her robe and lay it out on a rock to dry. Her two captors remained at a distance, for which she was grateful.

She never heard them talking about a ransom, and she wondered if anyone would ever find her. Earlier that morning, two dozen riders stopped at the cave to see her. She felt like an animal kept in a cage. They mocked her, calling her and her father names.

"Tomorrow night it will all be over, foul child of Khafre!" one shouted. The echo of his voice reverberated inside the cave.

"Let's do with her as we will," one of the riders yelled.

The leader of the group, at least she thought he might be the one, yelled, "No one is to touch her. Those are Herihor's orders!"

Herihor? Had she heard correctly?

She touched a dagger she had placed in her waist band. After the snake bite, her captors had given it to her for protection in the cave. She fantasized about overpowering them and stealing a horse for her escape to Giza.

When the band of assassins rode off, she wished she could jump on a horse and ride after them. *She* would find out who had abducted her.

On the day Pharaoh was to respond to the band of Djed's demand, an aide to the general arrived with a report. Khafre called in Hui to hear it as well.

The young warrior said, "Majesty, our men are advancing on the cave as we speak. Our archers will take out the guards and then rush the princess back to the ship. There is no reason for you to risk your life at Giza."

"No!" Pharaoh exclaimed. "They will only continue to threaten us. It will be Prince Dua next or my oldest son, and then my queen. I regret there are no other options, gentlemen. I am grateful for the report, Captain. Let us pray now that your rescue of the princess is successful."

"Majesty. Horus will be victorious!" the captain replied. He saluted, did an about face, and left the king's apartment.

Khafre walked outside on the veranda and Hui followed. "If they are successful Hui, we will be back where we were and so will they. We need to wipe them out once and for all. He was so angry, he swore again. "Seth's foul breath! I was looking forward to the fight. They'll disband and I'll have nothing to do but await another message or ransom note. I will be at their mercy." He walked to the railing and pounded it with his fist in frustration.

"The band must still be at Giza, Majesty," Hui said. "Can't the army attack them and round them up? We could send a messenger pigeon…" but then Hui stopped. "Of course, it's dark, they won't fly."

Pharaoh grew quiet. After a moment he said, "It's too late. If they learn of the attack on the cave, they'll flee and crawl back under the rocks they came from, like the vile creatures they are."

Prince Dua joined them and Hui brought him up to date on his sister's rescue.

"I pray Hettie will be safe, Father."

"Agreed. I rule this kingdom, and yet I am powerless."

Hui said, "We can only wait, my Lord. We'll leave you to your thoughts."

Khafre nodded as Hui and the prince left together.

Dua said, "This sounds insignificant compared to what's happening, but did Iset get along with Khensu?"

"Yes, she did. In fact, they got along very well. I am quite surprised. I learned from friends that the Mau can be quite violent. But they act like they grew up in the same litter."

Dua smiled. "Good. When you bring Iset to the palace now, she'll have a playmate."

"Indeed. You can watch them when your father and I have to travel."

Dua said, "I'll be glad when Hettie's back."

"I agree. I have to admit I've grown quite fond of her."

Dua grinned at him. "Yes, we know. Mother said you are in love with her. Is it true?"

Hui smiled. "In a way, I am. But why torture myself. It is a love doomed to fail. Your sister is a princess, and I only a poor cousin. The gods are against it."

"I wouldn't mind having you as a brother-in-law."

Hui laughed. "Thank you, Highness. We could raise our cats together."

It was Dua's turn to laugh. "Yes, we could. I hope to find a wife soon who likes cats."

"You'll have no trouble finding a wife, Prince. I've seen how the young ladies at court vie for your attention."

"There are plenty, but now I have to keep father from choosing a wife for me. . ."

"Give up that idea young man. It's what Pharaohs do."

In the cave's dark shadows, Hettie could not sleep. Tomorrow might be her last day in this life. Her captors would exchange her for the ransom, but if it wasn't paid, they would send her on her way to the afterlife.

An owl flew overhead, and then landed on the stump of an acacia near the cave entrance. It was probably looking for mice or small lizards. It hooted, and she found comfort in its soft call. Her ancestors believed that owls protected spirits as they passed from one world to the next. "Don't take me yet, owl. I still have a long life to live."

She looked at the bright stars above and her eyes followed a falling star. Her father had told her that they were gifts from the gods to earth. Pharaohs often buried them in their tombs. They were like metallic arrows, pointing the kings to the land of the gods.

"Get ready," she heard one of the guards call to the other. "We'll be moving her soon."

"Quiet, son of a toad! I'm trying to sleep," the other said.

"Shake a leg, Baka. The others will be along any moment."

"So you say."

They shuffled about, picking up their blankets and water-skins. The whinnying of horses reached her cave.

Abruptly, there was a loud swish and then another. Something flew through the air. One of her guards cried out, "I'm hit." Then there came the sound of the two horses neighing and moving about.

Another swish, and then another. More cries echoed in the night, and then all was silent. Only the frightened nickering of the horses trying to pull on their tether broke the silence.

The owl hooted again as it flew off.

CHAPTER NINETEEN

"Princess, you're alive!" A guardsman jumped off his horse and took her hand. "Come, we must ride. We don't have time for courtesies until we're back on the ship."

"I understand," Hettie said.

He helped her onto a horse. "Hold on, my Lady. Grab his mane and hug his neck if you need to."

"I'm all right," Hettie shouted.

They rode quickly away while the other guards cheered. Her heart pounded. She was going to make it back after all.

It wasn't a long ride, but before they reached the river, the guards took another road north until it came into view. Dawn was approaching and in the dim light, she recognized the ship.

"Bless the gods," she exclaimed.

When the crew on board saw her, they cheered and clapped. "Princess Rek-het-ray" they shouted over and over.

Two ladies-in-waiting hurried down the walkway to help her.

"Prepare a bath," she ordered. "All I can think of is that I must have half of the desert on me and in my hair."

The crew warmed the water for her. In her cabin, as she sank down into the copper tub, she closed her eyes and inhaled the fragrant perfumes her attendants poured into the water.

As she soaked, hoof beats galloping away from the ship reached her. Later, after drying off, the attendants put a new robe on her. She asked them, "Where have all the guards gone? Call the captain for me."

In response, a sergeant appeared on the royal deck. "Highness, how may I help you?"

"Where is your captain?"

"He's gone to join the rest of our forces at Giza, Highness. The other unit of guards and soldiers have attacked the band of Djed."

"Is Pharaoh with them?"

"His majesty is in Memphis, my Lady. General Haka is leading the attack. May Horus help them."

"Even so, Sergeant. What is your name?"

"I am Pubu, Highness."

"I am grateful, Sergeant, to you and your men. You saved me from a horrible death. Pharaoh will reward you for your courage."

"Finding you, Highness and discovering that you are all right is reward enough."

"Pharaoh will not agree, Sergeant. He will insist you and your men be recognized." She paused. "Will all our warriors come back here?"

"No, Highness. We will sail soon for Giza. If they are victorious, we'll pick them up. If not, we continue on to Memphis with you as planned."

"I understand. Thank you Sergeant. I know they will win."

"Horus is with us, Highness," Pubu said.

In Memphis, the sun had just come up and guards and servants were still changing shifts. A scribe ran down the hall of the palace and pounded on the outer door of Pharaoh's residence. "Majesty!" he shouted. "Majesty!"

Pharaoh's steward opened the door. "Quiet, you fool. What is it?"

"A message from Giza! Call his majesty."

Pharaoh ran out of his chamber wrapped in a sheet. He bellowed, "Why all this noise? What is it?"

"It's from Giza, Majesty," the scribe said, bowing and handing the small roll of papyrus to the king.

Khafre read it and shouted, "Hettie's safe! Praise the gods!"

The queen hurried out of their bedchamber and wanted to see the message. As she read, her eyes filled with tears and she collapsed onto one of the divans. "Thank Horus. She's going to be all right."

Khafre said, "Let us hope we will hear from General Haka soon."

The scribe nodded and left.

When Captain Geta, leader of the group that saved Hettie, arrived in Giza, he found General Haka's men in the river washing blood from their swords. Geta and his men rode up to the Great Lion and dismounted.

General Haka sat with his back against a column of the temple. One of his men was wrapping a bandage around his arm. "We have defeated them, Geta," Haka said.

"Praise Horus," the captain replied. "You are wounded, my Lord."

"It is nothing. Just a scratch. The princess? Is she safe?"

"Yes, General safe and on the ship. They should be arriving shortly."

"Good. Now go inside. You'll find the traitor Herihor, our prisoner."

Geta entered the sacred place with his men. The band of Djed lay everywhere on the granite floor. Most were killed by arrows, the rest by the sword. General Herihor sat on a bench, bound hand and foot with a cloth tied over his mouth. His eyes filled with hatred when he saw more of Haka's men had arrived.

Captain Ramei, one of the leaders of Haka's men nodded to Geta.

"How many were there?" Geta asked.

"Fifty foul sons of Seth," Ramei replied. He spat on the floor in front of Herihor. "May their Kas rest in darkness forever."

"I agree," Geta said. "What orders has the general given for their disposal?"

"They are to be cut up and thrown to the crocodiles," Ramei said. "Slaves are being brought to carry out the butchering."

"Sir," one of Geta's men ran toward him. "The general is asking for you."

Geta walked back outside and stood before the senior officer.

"Assemble the men, Captain. March them onto the cause-way to await the ship. They deserve to celebrate. Order plenty of beer."

Geta grinned. "Yes, General. Will you need a carrying chair, Sir?"

"What? It's my arm that's wounded, not my legs. You'll have to lead my horse, Captain."

"Of course, my Lord."

They didn't have long to wait. As the sun reached the top of the Great Pyramid, a lookout saw the sails of the ship and shouted, "She's coming."

Geta smiled. Both groups of warriors at the cave and at Giza had been successful. Pharaoh would be pleased. With the followers of Djed destroyed, they could no longer threaten Egypt.

When Haka's men saw the Princess standing at the railing waving to them, they pounded their shields. Geta watched their reaction as she walked down the walkway to greet them. They were taken by her beauty, and each man bowed his head to her as he went aboard. She smiled and nodded to them.

When General Haka came on board, she greeted him warmly. She fussed over him, making sure the bandage had been done right, ordering beer brought for him immediately.

Later, with his men settled in, Geta told them he had been impressed by the resilience of Pharaoh's daughter.

In her cabin, Hettie luxuriated in the life to which she had been accustomed. Her attendants brought food and wine, fresh bread and a small pot of honey.

The general, however, encouraged her to remain in the cabin until the ship sailed.

"You are too beautiful a distraction, Highness," he told her. "My men can't do their jobs. It will only be for a short time."

She laughed. "Very well, General and thank you for the compliment."

He saluted, and left the royal deck to join his men below.

Hettie reclined on her bed rubbing scented lotion into her hands. Her skin had become scratched and rough from the sand and rocks. The soldiers and crew shouted obscenities at the prisoner drawing her to the cabin window. They struck the heavy-set officer and spat on him as they took him below.

Hettie couldn't believe someone the family trusted had betrayed them. "Even that is too good for him," Hettie grumbled. He had taken the life of her beloved Paru and she hoped her father would pronounce the longest and most painful execution he could think of.

The ship's crew raised the anchors and Hettie went out on deck as they lowered the great sail. When it filled with wind, it made her think of the proud desert pheasant whose chest inflated when trying to attract a mate. The ship picked up speed with the current as it carried it north toward the delta and the Great Sea.

Captain Geta climbed the steps to her deck. "May I intrude, my Lady?"

He had been her rescuer, and she felt gratitude and relief toward him. "Of course." She was sitting on a cushioned divan, and motioned for him to sit on the bench opposite her. "I give you permission to sit, Captain."

The officer hesitated, and only sat on the edge of the bench. "I don't want to make you uncomfortable, Highness," he began. "But General Haka wants to know if they hurt you in any way."

Hettie looked away for a moment. When she turned back she said, "As evil as they were, they did not harm me—not physically anyway. A snake, one of those egg-eating ones, bit me in the cave, and they rushed me to a physician in Giza. They fed me and gave me water. They did not beat me, or hurt me whatsoever."

"Thank the gods for that, my Lady."

"Horus protected me, and the gods sent me an owl."

"An owl, Highness?"

"Yes, since they guard our Kas at death, I feared I would soon die."

"Yes, yes. I remember. We learned about it when we were children. The owl is a benevolent spirit, isn't it?"

"Yes. Why did it come to my cave just moments before you and your men arrived?"

"I think I know, Highness."

"Oh? Tell me."

"It was there to accompany the evil Kas of your abductors, my Lady. The owl comes only when there is a death, and the owl knew what was going to happen. I believe it."

"Of course. I should have thought of that. I'll never look at an owl the same again."

He stood. "I must return to the general, Highness. My men will now be jealous of me for being able to speak with you, and to sit in your presence. You have honored me."

"Being able to do so is a gift I give you forever, Captain. Wherever we are, you are permitted to sit with me."

Her remark unsettled the officer and he quickly made his way back down the steps.

One of her attendants approached. "He's quite good looking, that captain," the woman said. "Not that it's any of my business."

"No it is not," Hettie said. "You forget yourself. How are you called?"

"I am Aria, Highness. Benembra was my sister."

"Oh, I am so sorry, Aria." She got up, walked over to the woman and touched her arm. "I really liked her."

"Thank you, Highness. Pharaoh gave her a good burial, and my family is grateful."

Hettie lowered her eyebrows and made a stern face. "Well, if you want to serve me, you will have to learn not to be so curious."

Aria smiled. "Understood, and I'm sorry, my Lady. But I do think that officer is handsome. Such a body."

Forced to smile, Hettie said, "Enough. Bring me more wine. Have some yourself if you like."

"I will, Highness. Thank you."

The ship's crew unrolled a sailcloth awning over the royal deck. Hettie closed her eyes in the cool shade as a fresh breeze blew up and across her divan. The smell of the river was sweet as lotus flowers scented the air with their exotic fragrance. She dozed off and on. In one dream, she and Hui were kissing and her father barged in to arrest him. In another, she and her brother were standing in the temple of Horus. It was a wedding and Hettie was the bride. But every time she tried to see the face of the groom, she woke up.

"Highness," Aria said. "Would you like more bread?"

"Yes, and bring the honey too."

"Very good." Aria nodded and left.

When she finished eating, Hettie decided to take a promenade around the ship. She took the steps down to the main deck and the ship's captain came to meet her. He led her along the deck and she looked down at the oarsmen and smiled at them. The odor of sweat and unwashed bodies made her turn her head and walk to the railing. Inhaling deeply the fresh air, she continued along until she reached the bow.

"I love it up here, Captain. The view of the river is pleasant and the wind in my face invigorating."

"It's true, Highness. It's the best spot on the ship, unless you're up on the mast—that view is by far the best."

Hettie laughed. "I've only been up there once, Captain. If I remember, I had seen eight summers and thought I was invincible. I climbed to the top and became so afraid I couldn't come back down. My father had to send a crewman up to tie a rope around me and lower me. Humiliating."

The captain laughed with her. They walked astern and stood near the three large rudders.

"How much longer until we're home, Captain?"

"The sun will be just above the palm trees on shore, my Lady. We've still a good way to go."

Abruptly, and without warning, the ship struck something. Hettie almost lost her balance as the ship rocked back and forth.

"What was that?" she asked

"Over there, Highness," the captain said. He pointed to several large boulders in the middle of the river. When they began to move, she realized they'd struck a group of hippos.

"What must they weigh if they can cause a ship this large to lurch so violently?"

"They can capsize smaller ships, my Lady. I've seen it happen."

She stood for a moment studying the three rudder men steering the ship. She admired their muscles and how easily they could turn the large oars. She knew they rotated often because of the strength it took to steer the ship.

As she and the captain turned back to walk up the steps leading to her deck, one of the rudder men rushed forward and grabbed her. She screamed and the crew and guards rushed toward them.

"Back away," the crewman shouted.

Captain Geta and his men moved closer and looked at each other for instructions.

The man's arm around Hettie's neck tightened and she was having trouble breathing.

"Help me," she gasped.

"I do this in Dejdefre's name, our true Pharaoh. This princess is an abomination to Egypt. She is the daughter of Khafre the usurper."

Before he could speak again, Geta threw a dagger so fast and with such power, it struck and entered the man's skull between the eyes. His arm fell down releasing Hettie who collapsed on deck. Geta rushed to her side and helped her up.

"Forgive me for touching you, my Lady. I can't believe a crewman on this ship was one of the band of Djed."

Hettie stared down at her attacker. "There's the proof, Captain. Look at the base of his neck. It's the mark of the backbone of Osiris." She turned to the ship's company. "Throw him overboard. The crocodiles will have an early meal and may his Ka be cursed."

The men cheered her fierceness. They kicked the dead body and then tossed it out as far into the river as they could throw him.

"Will this ever end?" Hettie asked.

As if to answer her, a lonely falcon screeched as it swooped down and circled the mast of the ship.

"Horus has heard your prayer, Highness. He is watching over you." He paused and there was now a hint of a smile on Geta's face. "Mercifully, he didn't send an owl, but the protecting god of the Pharaohs."

Hettie smiled, and rubbed her sore neck. "He could have come a little sooner."

CHAPTER TWENTY

From the palace Hui could see a large crowd gathered at the docks. News of General Haka's victory at Giza spread through the capital. Hui's charioteer drove him in front of the royal family in a procession to the ship. He tried desperately to catch a glimpse of the princess.

As soon as Hui's chariot stopped at the walkway, he saw her standing on the upper deck watching her family approach. The roar of the crowd increased when they saw her.

The thrill of finding her made Hui's heart beat faster as he placed the reins of his horses in the hands of an aide. When Hui stepped out of his chariot, General Haka met him.

"Lord Chamberlain," the officer said, saluting with his good arm, fist to his chest. He escorted Hui up the blue carpet to the ship.

"Well done, General," Hui said. "His majesty is very pleased."

"Thank you, my Lord." He introduced Captains Geta and Ramei. "These are the two officers who won the day."

"We are grateful that Horus was with you and your men," Hui said. He glanced toward the royal deck as the princess descended the steps and waited. Trumpets announced the arrival of her parents and brother.

The crowd shouted as Prince Dua jumped out of his chariot and raced up the ramp. He climbed the steps and Hui smiled because instead of hugging his sister, he took her hand and kissed it.

Pharaoh drove his chariot with his queen at his side. The crowds pushed closer hoping to catch a glimpse of the royal couple as they approached the ship.

A little girl with a bouquet of flowers darted out in front of them.

Pharaoh saw the child in time and reined in the horses. The crowd quieted as Queen Persenet stepped out of the chariot and approached her.

The girl made a childish bow and handed the flowers to the queen. When her majesty accepted the bouquet, the people exploded into cheers and applause, shouting "Per-say-net," many times. The queen smiled as Pharaoh helped her step back into the chariot, flicked the reins and the royal couple rode on.

Upon reaching the carpet, Pharaoh helped his wife down. The instant Pharaoh's foot touched the ground everyone fell prostrate, holding their palms toward him. Soldiers and guards knelt on one knee and saluted. Like a door closing on a noisy room, total silence passed through the crowd.

Pharaoh raised his hand and the drums rolled—signaling for the people to stand. He walked up the ramp and stood with his arms crossed. The queen followed, and stood next to him.

Princess Hettie walked across the deck and bowed to her parents.

Khafre extended his arms and embraced her to the roaring approval of the crowd. "You have been in our thoughts. We praise Horus you are home."

"While in the cave, Father, I thought only of my family. I am pleased to be with you again."

Hui felt a lump in his throat when he saw tears fill Hettie's eyes as she embraced her father.

Hettie's mother kissed her and the crowd clapped their hands with delight.

The royal family left the ship and stepped into their chariots, Hettie riding with her brother. They rode back up the royal esplanade to the palace to the acclamation of the people.

Hui stood alone, staring at the procession as it disappeared in the distance.

The ship's captain turned to him. "The princess is quite a woman, my Lord, brave and courageous."

"Yes, she is, Captain, and we are grateful to you for bringing her back."

The crowd began to disperse as Hui walked down the ramp and stepped into his chariot. His driver flicked his thin whip at the horses as Hui ordered, "To the villa."

The charioteer nodded, and drove the horses away from the dock.

Iset awakened Hui and he rolled over in bed and picked her up. "Enough of your soft paws on my cheek, young lady. You know it works every time."

"Meow. . ."

He laughed. "Yes, and a good morning to you, too."

They walked into the kitchen and he placed her food on her dish. "I'm going to take my bath," he said.

"Meowlll…"

Ranofer, his steward, filled the bath with warm water and scented it with fragrant lotus blossoms.

Hui had no sooner entered the copper tub, than an urgent knock on the door reverberated through the house. His steward answered it, and hurried back to the bathing area in the garden.

"It's the princess, Master. She has let herself in."

"What?" Hui stood, forgetting where he was. "Throw me a towel, hurry!"

"Are you dressed?" Hettie asked as she walked into the garden.

Hui was so shocked he dropped his towel again, but hurriedly picked it up. "No, you can see I am not." He turned and walked from the garden to his bedchamber, grumbling as the princess followed him.

"But Hui, I've seen you naked before. Remember when we were in Abydos? We all went swimming in my grandfather's pool?"

Hui turned his back on her, put on his undergarment and then his kilt. Walking back out into the living room, he frowned at her. "Yes, but we were only eight summers old, Hettie. Allow me some modesty."

She chuckled. "You don't have anything to be ashamed of, Cousin."

Her comment made him grin, but he was still disappointed that she treated him so casually. "You treat Dua better than you do me. I thought you liked me."

"Of course I like you, old owl. You've always been like a brother to me." She paused and looked at him intently. "Yesterday you hurt me on the ship. Why didn't you welcome me back?"

"I was waiting for you to speak to *me*, Highness. But you chose not to."

"I nearly died out there, Hui. Didn't you care?" She sat on one of his divans and pouted.

He couldn't help smiling. She had been making that same face since she was little. He walked over and sat next to her. "I died a thousand deaths imagining what might have happened to you. I couldn't eat or sleep. These are not the emotions of a brother, Hettie."

Her closeness caused stirrings within him that he didn't want to deal with. The fragrance of her perfume made him dizzy and he made the mistake of looking into her eyes. He had to stand and move away.

"Meowwww…"

Iset ran and jumped onto Hettie's lap.

"Darling Iset," she said. "Did you know Hui, that Dua has a cat? It looks very much like yours."

Disappointed she would change the subject, he nodded. "He left Khensu here and the cats get along very well. Better than we expected." He looked directly at her. "I wish it were true of us."

Hettie petted Iset and then let her down. "You'll preside at the ceremony of tribute for the guards and the army tomorrow won't you?"

He nodded.

"So perhaps you'll stay for the mid-day meal with us."

"Only if Pharaoh invites me."

She sighed. "But aren't you family, Hui?"

"Yes."

"You are as royal as any of us. Princesses have been known to marry their cousins with Pharaoh's approval."

Hui stood and felt his face flush. "Well, since you approve of my body, does that mean you could accept me as your husband?"

Hettie stood and moved toward him. For a moment, she just walked her fingers up and down his bare arm, and then her eyes sought his. "In that horrible cave, I dreamed about you. In my fear and loss of everything and everyone I held dear, I couldn't get you out of my mind. I even saw a spirit owl and it reminded me of you. When we are close to each other, it is as if my whole being is coming to life."

Hui's body, quivered. "I never hoped, Hettie, that you could love me. When I'm around you, my body goes mad."

She whispered, "I know what you mean."

They embraced and their scents mingled, their lips met and pressed together with a hunger held back for too long. Desire threatened to control him. He released her and stepped back, holding her at arm's length. The play of light and shadow in the room made Hettie seem lovelier than ever. Mysterious and sublime, she was happiness itself. She wore a simple white pleated gown and the skin of her upper body, caressed by the sun, was the color of oiled cedar wood. Her breasts were firm and supple. The slant of her eyes revealed a silver-green eye shadow.

Unable to breathe, he gasped, "Oh, my beloved, I've dreamed of doing this for the longest time."

"The gods have brought us together," she said, her voice trembling with desire.

Iset sat looking at them in the strangest way. "Meow?. . ."

"Yes, Iset," Hui said. "I love her. Do you approve?"

The cat walked around their legs rubbing against them and mewling.

Hui picked her up. "She does, she's purring her heart away."

The celebration began the next day with the entire court assembled in the Hall of Audiences.

The Lord Chamberlain commanded silence by tapping the polished granite floor with his staff.

"Behold the Daughter of Pharaoh, Princess Rekhetre—*She Who Sees Horus*."

The courtiers prostrated themselves, turning their palms toward her as she entered. She walked nobly forward and stood next to her mother's throne.

Hui reacted to her nearness and cleared his throat. "Bow before the Son of Pharaoh, Prince Duaenre—*He Who Follows Horus*. Crown Prince and Heir to the Sacred Throne."

Dua entered and stood next to his father's throne.

"Bow before Her Majesty, Queen Persenet, Principal wife of Khafre and Daughter of Iset, Mother of Egypt and the Heir to the throne."

The queen entered as the courtiers remained on the floor. Each gesture Persenet made was perfect. Each pose seemed to come from some brilliant painter who captured the ideal beauty in the body of this woman. She walked, head held high, and stood in front of her throne.

A fanfare of trumpets responded as Hui raised his staff again and tapped three times. "Bow low before Pharaoh Khafre—the Son of Horus, and Living God of Egypt. The Great Bull and Father of the Land."

Another blast of trumpets accompanied Khafre as he walked majestically up to his throne and took his queen's hand. As they sat down at the same time, he gestured for the people to stand. He spoke to them in a loud voice.

"Lord Chamberlain, call forth those to be honored."

Hui called Captain Ramei to stand forth. The officer walked in and knelt on one knee in front of their majesties. Next, he called Captain Geta and Sergeant Pubu who knelt beside their comrade.

Pharaoh stood. "You warriors are responsible for rescuing our beloved daughter, and for defeating the band of Djed. We honor you and your troops this day." He nodded to Hui who came forward with three flat cedar boxes. He opened the first, and Pharaoh took out a gold necklace with a small bar of gold hanging from it.

"Captain Ramei, receive the Gold of Valor from us and a grateful people."

The courtiers clapped and the soldiers in the hall stomped their feet. It sounded like drumming as it echoed around the great room.

"Captain Geta, receive the Gold of Valor from a grateful father and mother for rescuing the princess." As he placed the necklace around the young officer's neck, he whispered, "There will soon be an increase of pay for your bravery."

Geta, too moved to respond, simply nodded and saluted once more.

"Sergeant Pubu, our daughter has told us of your bravery at the cave. Receive this Gold of Valor with our gratitude." As he placed the necklace around the sergeant's neck, he whispered, "There will soon be a promotion for your actions."

Hui tapped the floor again, and the men stood, did an about face and walked back to join their company.

Pharaoh nodded to his chamberlain who signaled for the drummers to begin a long drumroll.

Hui raised his voice. "Great Pharaoh. Receive General Haka, Commander of the Army of the North."

Haka entered and knelt before the king.

Pharaoh walked down the steps and stood in front of the veteran officer. “Stand, my Lord. Receive from your Pharaoh the Gold of Victory.”

Hui walked toward them with another cedar box. He opened it and Khafre removed the necklace and placed it over the general’s head.

The courtiers cheered and Haka’s men stomped with approval.

The king spoke so only the general and Hui to hear. “We will name you Chief of Generals, and High Commander of Pharaoh’s Armies. We are grateful, Commander.”

Pharaoh turned to address the court. “It is our decree that the guards and soldiers who defeated the evil band of Djed and rescued Princess Rekhetre each be given ten pieces of gold and promotion in rank. Their names will be inscribed on a marble stele placed between the mighty paws of the Great Lion at Giza.”

The throne room filled with thunderous cheering and stomping.

Pharaoh extended his hand toward the queen, who stood and walked to him. They joined hands.

Hui tapped the floor, and the people made obeisance a last time. The military knelt and saluted. When the royal family had gone, Hui tapped again so the courtiers could stand.

As they dispersed, he approached Captain Geta. “As a personal friend of the princess, I want to thank you for risking your life to save her. We will remember your service.”

Embarrassed, Geta shuffled his feet and nodded. He thanked the chamberlain and left the hall.

When Hui arrived at the palace, he carried Iset with him. She and Dua's cat played as if they were kittens. Pharaoh enjoyed them and laughed at their antics.

"It's as if they were from the same litter," he said.

Dua nodded. "I said the same, Father."

The family took their places around the table as servants brought in steaming bowls of freshly baked fish, corn, leeks and a small basket of warm bread.

Hui smiled when the queen warned Hettie not to talk about her privations in the cave. "It would not be appropriate at the table, my dear."

Pharaoh did not allow talk about political issues, so Hui helped guide the conversation to the restoration of the face of the Great Lion.

"You've seen it most recently Princess," he said. "How does it look?"

Hettie looked at him and then at her father. "It's magnificent, Father. It looks just like you. Did you tell them to change the face to your image?"

"No," and he paused. "But it is true, however, that I do resemble my father, Khufu. We remember his name."

The family recited, "Khufu's sacred name is remembered."

Khafre continued. "You can see it on the paintings of him everywhere. I cannot change this face. I am who I am. Only the gods can change it."

"Well, I like your face, Father," Hettie said.

"Good. I'd hate for the sculptors to have to change the lion's face all over again. The Lion is very fragile. It is already more than a thousand summers old. My wise men say it is older than Egypt itself."

Dua said, "I can't begin to imagine anything that old."

Persenet said, 'I've heard one of my attendants speaking about you, Son. She said the king of Byblos is seeking a prince to marry his daughter."

"Mother, I will choose a wife for myself. Besides, I want an Egyptian wife."

His father said, "What made you think you could decide something that important on your own, my Son? The woman I will choose is a matter of state."

Dua frowned. "I thought it was a matter of the heart, Father."

"Not when you will be Pharaoh, Dua."

Hettie spoke up. "What about a prince for me, Father. Do you have any prospects?"

"The gods have not been kind to you, Hettie."

"What if I were to find a nobleman you approve of. Could I marry him?"

"It would depend on the man."

Hettie's mother said, "He would have to be good, kind, and love you very much."

Hettie nodded. "I agree, Mother."

Dua looked at Hui with a knowing look. A sly smile reached his lips and he nodded ever so slightly.

That made Hui nervous. He hoped Dua wouldn't say anything. "Shall I leave Iset here, Majesty? She seems happiest when she is with you."

"Certainly. Khensu will be happy too, Nephew."

Pleased of the reminder that he was part of the family, he said, "Then I will take my leave, Majesty. Thank you for inviting me to your table."

"Thank Hettie, it was her idea," Khafre said.

"Thank you Princess. I will bid you good night."

Iset followed him to the door. Hettie walked over and picked her up.

"Good night, my Heart," she whispered."

"And to you, Queen of my dreams."

When Hui turned, he found Dua staring at the two of them.

"You certainly are in love. The way you look at each other. I'm surprised Mother hasn't figured it out."

"Quiet, little weasel," Hettie whispered. "One word to anyone and I'll have someone kidnap you!"

Hui grew even more nervous. "My life is in your hands, Dua. I have loved your sister since I was a child. I believe she loves me too. Don't allow your father to pick anyone else for her. Let her marry someone she truly loves."

Dua walked closer. "You have nothing to fear from me, Cousin. When I become Pharaoh, I will want as my chamberlain someone I can call friend. Now goodnight. Let us pray we find a way to convince father."

When the prince left them, Hui and Hettie embraced and kissed good night. He held her tightly, afraid the beautiful creature might fly away like a goddess returning to the heavens.

"You are my sun," she whispered. "My day is dark without you."

He sighed. "You are the river of my heart. The waters of your love feed my soul."

"You are my chosen spouse, in this world and all the worlds to come."

"And you are mine, and I pledge you my love."

Iset meowed as Hui reluctantly released Hettie's hand and left the palace.

CHAPTER TWENTY-ONE

Three months passed as Hui and Hettie's love grew stronger. Before the statue of Horus in the family altar, her brother swore an oath to keep their secret.

Pharaoh's preoccupation however, was the upcoming dedication of the completed repairs on the Great Lion a week away. They would sail together to Giza for the ceremony.

Hui left Memphis earlier to insure the arrangements would be ready. When he returned, he reported to his majesty that the face of the Great Lion was completed and assured Khafre he would be pleased.

"The great statue has never looked this good, Majesty," he said. "And the temple beneath it has been purified and prepared for the worship of Horus on the day of the dedication."

"Well done, Hui. You honor your father by your attention to detail. You have become a good chamberlain."

"A great compliment, Majesty. I am humbled by your words."

"Will everything on the galley be ready?"

"Yes, Great One. Your newest ship in the fleet, the *Wings of Horus,* will take you."

"Good, Captain Mered is a capable man."

"He is eager for you to come aboard."

Khafre was silent for a moment. "Is the high priest going to arrive ahead of us?"

"Yes, Lord Horirem said he wants to make sure the musicians and chorus of priests are in place and ready for the ceremony."

Khafre nodded. "I am unsure about the ceremony itself. The people must be aware that these special events all seem the same. They need more excitement."

"I would propose, Majesty," and then Hui quickly stopped and corrected himself. "I cannot tell Pharaoh what to do, but this is something you might consider. Cover the Lion's face with a large sailcloth to keep its beauty a surprise for those who attend. The orchestra and chorus could assemble on the Lion's back, ready for the unveiling before you speak."

"Yes, go on."

"The artists could paint your father's cartouche on the cloth, large enough for everyone to see and will leave no doubt as to whose face it is."

"Excellent."

"The high priest could then bless the Lion while you turn and face your father's image. At that moment, Majesty, you will pull the cord to reveal the work your artists have done. Hundreds of white doves will be released, flying up into the sky reminding us of the flight of Great Khufu's Ka into the afterlife."

Khafre smiled. "The people will love it, Hui. Do not tell anyone else what we have planned. We will surprise the family and guests."

"As you command, Majesty. I would also add that the ceremony in the temple is entirely in the hands of the high priest. Does that please you?"

"Yes. Lord Horirem is very formal and expects his priests to know what they are doing at all times."

"I like him," Hui said.

"He told me he is concerned about you, Hui."

"For me, Majesty?"

"Yes. He says you are in love with my daughter, and that it will only break your heart when she is given to another."

Stunned, Hui swallowed hard, and was at a complete loss for words.

"Do you love Hettie, Hui?"

"Majesty, you know I have loved her since I was eight. I never dreamed she could be mine. Now, as a family member, and being so close to her every day, tears me apart." He paused and looked directly at the king. "You may have me executed, Uncle, but her love is what keeps me alive."

"I do not blame you for loving her, Hui. But I am not sure as my nephew the court would approve such a marriage."

"Yes, my Lord, but forgive my impertinence. As Pharaoh, Majesty, you are the law of the land. What you decide becomes law. I am your sister's son. But for now, if you allow it, I am content just to be near her."

Pharaoh didn't respond and Hui bowed his head slightly, before leaving the king's apartment.

Hui found Hettie in the royal family's sitting room.

"What do you mean father knows about us?" she demanded.

"He came out and asked me directly if I loved you."

"And what was your answer?"

"I said that he has known since we were children that I love you. It is the truth, Hettie and I can't deny it."

"What did he do?"

"Well, I'm alive, but I don't know what he will do. I reminded him that I am his nephew."

A silence fell between them as they sat on separate divans.

Iset wandered in and ignored them both.

"There is something wrong with her," Hui said. "She's been acting strangely."

Hettie walked over and the cat growled. "Iset, what is it?" She turned back toward Hui. "You're feeding her too much."

"Where's Khensu?" he asked.

Hettie frowned. "I don't know. For some reason Iset won't let him come around. Serves him right."

The new royal galley sailed for Memphis with great fanfare and cheers from the crowd. Hui had chosen blue in all its variations for the ship's long streamers that floated above the vessel. The blues of the sky and the river in the sunlight, the blues of the petals of the desert orchid and the shimmering blue of the river perch. He chose his favorite colors of red and yellows for the banners of Pharaoh's canopy in front of his cabin.

It took the *Wings of Horus* two days to reach the causeway leading up to Khufu's monuments. A large crowd had assembled and souvenir sellers were already hawking small statues of the Great Lion.

"I do not know what all the fuss is about. It is only a statue," the queen said.

"But Mother," Hettie said. "It is the biggest statue in the world."

The queen frowned. "Bigness does not mean it is good."

Once Pharaoh's ship docked at the causeway, no other ships could anchor. The royal family was living aboard and therefore access to the causeway was restricted.

Hui and Prince Dua went ashore to ascertain if the high priest and participants in the ceremony were ready.

"I like the large cloth hiding the lion's face," Dua said. "It adds mystery to the occasion. Father is brilliant, is he not?"

Hui smiled. "Yes, Highness, he is,"

At their meeting with the High Priest, Hui sensed he was very nervous. "Why are there so many people here?" Lord Horirem said. "I am not sure I can do this in front of so many."

"Ignore them, my Lord. You are here to please only two people—Pharaoh, Horus' son on earth, and the mighty god himself."

"You're right of course. I'm just concerned, Hui, forgive me. Is everything ready for tomorrow? Are all the musicians here?"

"Yes, my assistant has counted everyone, my Lord. They arrived earlier in the week and have camped near the Great Pyramid. Don't worry."

Hui said, "Remember the *Hymn to Horus* is a special presentation for the king. It is important they sing loudly."

"Understood." Horirem excused himself and went to check on the other priests.

That evening, the servants served the royal family on the upper deck of the ship. They took their places at a large table brought on board from one of the temples in Giza. Torches placed at intervals around the royal family were there to chase away insects. Servants held large ostrich fans which drove away the rest who avoided the flames. As the sun slipped slowly behind the Great Pyramid, it drew everyone's eyes to the west.

"Look how the electrum at the summit of the pyramid shines," the queen said. "And the sides of the pyramid facing the setting sun appear to turn to gold in Ra's light."

"It's glorious," Hui said.

When the food arrived, Hui felt as if he'd already passed into the afterlife without having to die. So much food was overwhelming. Earlier that afternoon, the king's archers went hunting, and the roasted antelope on the table was their gift in Pharaoh's honor. The venison was tasty, as were all the other culinary delights.

At the meal's end, the family made their way to their cabins. Hettie remained at the railing, enjoying the sky as it changed from magenta to purple, to deep black. A full moon made it easy for Hui to admire her face.

"May Horus be with you tomorrow, my Love," she said.

"Thank you, Highness. To have you here is all the good fortune I need."

Prince Dua came up behind them. “Better keep you two apart. I do not mean to spoil the moment, but father is not in bed yet. He could come on deck at any time.”

Hettie scowled at him. “All right, Dua, you have made your point.” She turned to Hui, “Good night, Beloved. Sweet dreams.”

“They will be,” Hui said. “They’re always of you.”

Dua remained next to Hui. “Promise you’ll take care of her, Cousin.”

“I will, Prince. I’m glad you approve.”

“You two are well-suited. You like and even laugh at the same things. You tolerate me which is amazing.”

Hui grinned. “I have to, Dua. You will be Pharaoh someday.”

“And do not forget it,” Dua said as he grinned and left him.

Inside his cabin, Hui stood by the open window. He inhaled the sweet fragrance of the water as it rushed past the ship. Moonlight made sparkling patterns on the black surface, interrupted only by the shadowy figure of a hippo swimming past.

“Meow…” Iset whispered.

“And little lady, you are sleepy aren’t you?” He removed his kilt and stretched out on the bed. Iset snuggled up to him and he rubbed her back for a long time. Her purring soothed his nerves and he closed his eyes.

A rooster somewhere in Giza awakened him the next morning. He yawned, stretched his arms over his head and walked to the window. Guardsmen were moving about on deck and Captain Geta saw him and waved. Hui called for his steward to prepare his bath. The man brought in a copper tub, which the servants of the royal family filled with warm water. When he finished, he dressed and shut Iset inside, closing the window to be certain she wouldn't get out.

Captain Geta climbed the steps to the royal deck. "When does the ceremony begin, my Lord, or should I say Prince or Highness?"

Hui felt his face turn red. "'Prince', may be proper, Geta, but 'Lord' is more comfortable. The ceremony will begin when you hear the king's trumpeters."

Hui left the ship and took one last walk through all his preparations. When he returned, the moment arrived. He worried when he thought Iset had gotten out of the cabin, but he found her under his bed. "Why are you hiding, little one? Oh, well. Stay there. I don't have time for you now." He put on his gold and turquoise-striped nemes headdress and walked on deck to meet with Pharaoh.

Trumpets announced the ceremony's beginning. Pharaoh's guards and Haka's soldiers lined both sides of the causeway. Hui would lead the procession. Instead of riding in their golden chairs, Pharaoh, the queen and their children would walk to the temple. It wasn't far, and Khafre liked to be near his people.

Upon reaching the steps leading down to the temple under the Great Lion, a group of priests met their majesties and led them inside for the service.

After the high priest's short ceremony and prayers to Horus, Horirem led the royals back outside and up to the front of the Great Lion. Steps, built for the occasion out of wood, would enable the king, high priest and chamberlain to stand beneath the beard of the Lion's face.

Lord Horirem led them up the steps and the three men stood facing the crowd. A loud fanfare sounded, and the high priest began an incantation bestowing blessings on the Great Lion and the image of Khufu, builder of the Great Pyramid. The *Hymn to Horus* sung by the priests echoed over the plateau.

Hui looked up above the head and checked to make sure the cord was in place for the unveiling of the face. A slight wind blew the canvas cloth, and the movement added to the mystery of what was happening.

Finally, it was Khafre's turn to speak. He addressed the crowd in a loud voice and declared the official dedication of the Lion Protector of Pharaoh Khufu.

The crowd shouted Khafre's father's name three times---"Khoo-foo"—each time louder than the first.

Pharaoh smiled and turned to face the Lion, as did Hui and the high priest. His majesty pulled on the cord, and the large cloth with his father's name on it fell slowly away from the face. The crowd gasped and Hui could hear their exclamations of surprise. The people clapped and cheered and sang the song they had sung at Khufu's entombment.

Khafre was pleased. His smile became a grin as he turned back to face the people.

Abruptly, a strange sound Hui had never heard before, came from above. He looked up as the large nose of the face cracked and slid down over the mouth—falling toward Pharaoh. Hui didn't think, but reacted and grabbed Pharaoh and pulled him away as the nose struck Hui and pushed him off the platform. Something snapped in his leg and he cried out.

The high priest had also fallen to the floor of the platform, but he stood and brushed dust from his robe.

"Majesty!" Hui yelled. "Are you all right?"

Khafre coughed, then picked himself up. He looked down at Hui and rushed to his side.

"You have saved my life again, Hui! By the gods!"

Hui winced in pain. He couldn't move his right leg. One of the giant stones of the nose had struck it scraping off the skin. Blood oozed from the wound.

Dua and Hettie rushed up the steps.

Pharaoh shouted for his physician and the healer hurried to the wounded chamberlain.

Pharaoh said, "He will take you to the ship, Hui. You will be alright."

The pain became so intense, Hui almost passed out.

Pharaoh grabbed his arm and repeated, “I owe you my life.”

Hui awoke in his cabin two days later. Hettie was holding his hand.

“Ow,” he cried out abruptly as pain struck him. His leg was encased in a cast of tightly-wound linens covered in plaster. The throbbing forced him to grit his teeth.

“Easy son, drink this,” the king’s physician ordered. “It’ll help the pain.”

Queen Persenet sat on the other side of his bed. “You are a hero, Lord Chamberlain. You’ve saved my husband. We’ve seen that you’ve had the best care. Your leg has been set and the physician says the bone will heal nicely.” She put her hand on his shoulder. “Thank you, Hui.”

“Majesty,” was all Hui could say. He still felt nauseous and a little groggy.

“What is that strange noise,” he asked. “That strange trilling sound?”

Hettie went over to a box on the other side of the cabin. She reached inside, picked something up and walked back to his bed.

“Kittens, my Lord. Iset and Khensu have given us kittens!”

Hui laughed at the little cat and then closed his eyes as the drug took full effect.

The next day, he had a visitor.

Pharaoh entered his room and sent everyone out.

Hui tried to bow, but Khafre wouldn't allow it.

"It is I who should bow to you, Hui. I could have died up there. In fact, we all could have been killed. I've executed the sculptors who carved the face. It was a stupid accident. The sandstone gave way and the nose almost took us with it."

"Yes, my Lord."

"I've come to reward you for saving me."

"I don't understand, Majesty."

"I will give you anything you want, my boy. The life of Pharaoh is worth something. What do you want?"

"You won't give it, Great One."

"I swear before my ancestors and all the gods. Whatever you want will be yours."

Hui did something never allowed by anyone except family—he looked into Pharaoh's eyes. "The hand of your daughter, Great Pharaoh. Allow your nephew to marry Hettie. After all, I am a grandson of the Great Khufu."

Pharaoh stood and put his hands behind his back, rocking on his heels a moment. When he stopped, he leaned in closer to the young man. "On my word as ruler of this land I give Princess Rekhetre to you in marriage."

Having listened at the door, Hettie burst in and looked at her father. He smiled and nodded to her. "He's yours my dear, if you still want him."

She hugged her father and he turned and left the cabin.

Hettie sat beside Hui and they embraced gently. She offered her face to him and he kissed her, deeply and the kiss lingered. They hugged again, until Hui winced in pain.

"Meowrlll..." a voice cried from the floor. Iset jumped up and snuggled between the two of them. She began to purr and Hettie scratched her under the chin.

Hui stretched his arms and crossed them behind his head. The smile on his face was the biggest he ever had. Iset mewed again and reached up and patted his nose.

Outside the cabin, Prince Dua announced the news of the princess' betrothal to the ship's company. Their cheers and stomping rocked the boat.

The crew lowered the great sail, and Hui felt the surge of the ship as it moved forward toward home.

Dua's cat, meowed and Iset jumped down from the bed and sat beside him. He licked her cheek and she closed her eyes in contentment.

From the cabin window, Hettie pointed to something in the sky. "Oh, Hui, can you see?"

Careful not to move his injured leg, he leaned over to look. "Ah," he said.

Soaring above the ship on warm thermals from the cliffs, two majestic falcons cried out and dove toward the vessel. To everyone's surprise, they landed on the spar holding the sail and rubbed their beaks together. The crew lifted their arms and cheered.

"It's a sign," Hettie said.

"Indeed, beloved. Horus is blessing our union."

She walked back to the bed and sat beside him. He pulled her to him gently and they kissed, oblivious of the excited happy laughing of the crew on deck.

A gentle breeze blew through the window—its sweet fragrance of lotus blossoms permeated the cabin with an incense-like blessing from the gods.

On the floor beside the bed, Iset curled next to Khensu, and their contented purring filled the room with joy.

The End

Made in the USA
Middletown, DE
07 May 2019